Follow Your Heart

And

Other Stories

CONTENTS

FOLLOW YOUR HEART

Lisa Quinn spent the morning at the office where she worked in Lower Manhattan, joined two colleagues for lunch at a nearby restaurant and had just returned to her desk, when the telephone rang. Usually it was just a matter of answering the phone and putting the call through to her boss or one of the other executives who worked in the building. She was taken aback, therefore, when the person on the other end of the line asked if he could speak to her.

"This is Lisa Quinn speaking".
"Oh, hello Lisa, nice to speak to you at last".
Lisa was puzzled. "Who am I speaking to?"

she asked, nervously.

"My name is Matthew Donnelly and I'm calling from Ireland."

Lisa thought he said he was ringing from Ireland, but she wasn't at all sure as he had a weird accent and she had difficulty understanding him. Perhaps he was a crank caller; how was she to know? She had heard stories of people receiving such calls before, so without allowing him to say another word, she put down the phone and got on with her work for the remainder of the afternoon.

It was only when Lisa was on her way home that evening to Brooklyn where she lived with her mother that she had time to think again about the strange phone call and she wondered if she'd done the right thing. It wasn't as if she had no connection, whatsoever, with Ireland. Her paternal grandparents had emigrated from there New York in the late eighteen hundreds but had both passed away before she was born. With her father dying suddenly when she was only five years old, and her mother being of Italian descent, she knew practically nothing about her Irish roots.

Lisa's father had been a successful businessman and when he died he left Lisa and her mother well-off. As she was an only child her mother always made sure she had the best of everything including a good education. While she was still at school she met her first and only boyfriend, William. Lisa's mother greatly approved of William, especially as he was a member of an equally successful business family with a bright future ahead of him. On her twenty-fifth birthday they got engaged and the wedding was due to take place in six months. Recently however, Lisa was beginning to have some niggling doubts. She often felt that she had allowed her relationship with William to just drift along. Perhaps it was her mother's enthusiasm rather than hers that was keeping the romance alive. However, she couldn't see herself backing out now; it would be too upsetting for everyone.

Before she went to sleep that night, however, she made up her mind that if the person who said he was from Ireland called again, this time she'd at least see what he had to say. After all, it could be something to do with her relatives in Ireland. As it turned out, she didn't have long to wait. The following day the phone rang at around the same time in the afternoon. After apologising for getting cut off the previous day, Mr. Donnelly went on to explain that he was a solicitor who was contacting her regarding the last will and testament of her grand-aunt, Miss Elizabeth Quinn, who had passed away three months previously in her ninety-third year. Miss Quinn had left her house and thirty-two acres of land in County Galway to her grand-niece, Lisa.

Lisa was stunned by this unexpected news. She asked the solicitor if he was sure there wasn't some mistake. Surely, Miss Quinn must have had some relatives in Ireland who would be more entitled to this legacy than her. Mr. Donnelly assured her there was no mistake. She was definitely the person named in the will; there could be no doubt about that.

"There is, however, a condition attached to the bequest. Miss Quinn stipulated that before the property can be transferred into your name you must live in it for a period of three months. When that time is up you can either continue to live there or sell up lock, stock and barrel and return to America; the choice is yours."

"Live in it for three months! That's the craziest thing I ever heard!" Am I to give up everything and travel across the Atlantic Ocean to take up residence in God only knows what sort of a shack in the middle of nowhere? I'm sorry, but I don't think so, Mr. Donnelly."

"Well Lisa, I'm afraid that's the deal. I understand your concern about having to put your life on hold and travel to a strange country, but perhaps you could look on it as an adventure, something to tell your grandchildren about in years to come."

Before they finished their conversation Lisa told Mr. Donnelly that, rather than make a hasty decision, she'd take a week to think it over, and then she'd let him know what she wished to do, and he promised to ring her back the following week. When she put down the phone she thought, I must be mad to agree to even consider this proposition. For the remainder of the afternoon, however, she couldn't stop thinking about it and had great difficulty concentrating on her work. She was glad when five o'clock finally arrived so she could down tools and head for home.

Later that evening during dinner, Lisa told her mother about the phone call. At first she understood it was just a matter of a house in Ireland being sold and the proceeds being sent on to her daughter. Wouldn't it be a nice little windfall for Lisa, she thought, especially now with her wedding only six months away? However, when she heard about the condition attached she was dumbfounded.

"But that's ridiculous," she exclaimed, "Surely you told him you're not interested."
"Well … I didn't actually, I said I'd think about it."
"Think about it? Are you mad? You do realise you have a wedding to prepare for. And what about William? What's he going to think of his fiancé going off on a wild goose chase across the Atlantic a few months before your

wedding?"

Lisa didn't dare say it to her mother, but the thought crossed her mind that she didn't really care what William thought. In any case, the wedding was six months away. If she left for Ireland soon she could still be back in plenty of time to get married – if she still wanted to. Over the following days she spent a lot of time thinking things over. Perhaps this was the opportunity she needed to take control of her life and future instead of always going along with what others decided for her. By the end of the week she had made up her mind; she was going to Ireland, everything else could wait.

Two weeks later, on a cool but sunny morning in early April, nineteen seventy-one, the plane carrying Lisa Quinn and two hundred other passengers touched down safely at Shannon Airport. Lisa was thankful that at least the first leg of her journey was over. From the airport she took a bus to Galway city and another on to the town of Tuam. When at twelve o'clock she stood outside the offices of *Matthew Donnelly &*

Company, Solicitors, she allowed herself to breathe a sigh of relief. It was hard to believe that, despite never having travelled alone before in her life, she had made it this far without any hitches, and she said a silent prayer that the rest of her journey would be equally stress free.

When she entered the office Mr. Donnelly was delighted to see her and, with a *céad míle fáilte* and a hearty handshake, welcomed her to Ireland. The rest of the day passed by in a blur there was so much information to take in. She stayed in Tuam that night and the following morning the solicitor drove her out to the house in his car. Before leaving the town she bought enough provisions to last her for a day or two; after that she would do her shopping in the local village.

As the roads narrowed and the countryside became more rugged Lisa wondered if they were ever going to reach their destination. Eventually, after passing through a small village called Donore, they continued for another two miles and turned down a winding boreen. Suddenly, they rounded a bend and there it was: a small stone house with a slated roof, a red front door and four windows with tiny panes of glass. The yard had its fair share of grass and weeds with a selection of outhouses around the perimeter. Lisa had never seen anything like it.

"Well Lisa, what do you think?" asked Mr. Donnelly.

"It's … nice, I suppose," replied Lisa, uncertainly, "but I didn't expect it to be so isolated. Do you really think it's safe to stay here on my own?"

"Of course it's safe. I know this area well and there has never been any trouble around these parts. You'll have my phone number anyway, if you have any problems you can give me a ring from the phone box in the village."

After he had taken her into the house and shown her where to find everything she needed, Mr. Donnelly bid her goodbye and left. As Lisa stood at the door watching the car disappear around the bend, she couldn't help wondering if she was doing the right thing. The solicitor had said she could ring him from the village: a fat lot of good that would do her if someone broke into the house in the middle of the night! However, she told herself to calm down. Hadn't he said the place was safe; she'd just have to take him at his word. So after a bite to eat and a quick poke around, she said she'd have an early night as she was exhausted after all the travelling of the past few days.

The following morning after breakfast Lisa decided to take a walk into the village. If she was to stay here she'd have to get to know her neighbours, and now was as good a time as any to make a start. As she made her way across the yard she spotted a bicycle lying against the wall of one of the outhouses. On closer inspection it appeared to be in good condition, although a bit rusty in places and the front tire was flat. Luckily, there was a pump attached so without too much difficulty she pumped up the tire, then hoisted herself up on the saddle and wobbled off unsteadily in the direction of the village.

Less than an hour later, having purchased a few items that she needed in Flynn's Grocery & Hardware Store, and answered Mrs. Flynn's numerous questions about who she was and where she came from, Lisa set out on her return journey. She hadn't gone very far when she noticed that the front tire of the bicycle was flat again. She tried pumping it up but it was no use. Oh no, she thought, not only will I have to walk all the way, but I'll have to push this useless article as well. After trudging along for about fifteen minutes she heard a noisy vehicle coming along the road behind her. Afraid of getting knocked down she stood into the ditch holding the bicycle in front of her. A tractor and trailer roared passed but stopped a few yards from where she stood.

"Are you in trouble?" asked the young man in the driver's seat.

"It's just the bicycle," replied Lisa, "It seems to have a puncture and I have to push it home."

"I can give you a lift, if you like. Have you far to go?"

"No, I'm staying at the house that used to belong to Elizabeth Quinn. Do you know it?"

The young man smiled. "Lizzy Quinn's place

– of course I know it! Sure I only live a few yards down the road. By the way, I'm Eoin McDermott, what's your name?

"Lisa" she told him, "Lisa Quinn."

Eoin lifted the bicycle onto the trailer, Lisa climbed on and sat down beside it, and soon they were on their way. She was nervous at first as she had never seen a tractor and trailer up close before not to mention getting a lift on one. However, she soon got used to the noise and enjoyed the feel of the wind on her face as they chugged along. When he dropped her off at the end of the boreen she thanked him for his help. Then, hopping back on his tractor and giving her a friendly wave he disappeared around the bend. "Hmm," thought Lisa, as she pushed the bicycle down the boreen, "What a nice fella, not bad-looking either, I wonder when I'll see him again."

As it happened, she didn't have long to wait. The following evening Eoin drove up to the house in his battered old Fiat 850 and offered to fix the bicycle for her. She was delighted, and when he was finished she invited him in for a cup of tea. They chatted for a while and when he left she was already looking forward to seeing him again. A few days later he called again and asked her if she'd like to go to the pub in the village on Friday; there'd be a band playing, he said, and it should be a terrific night. Lisa wasn't sure whether he was asking her on a date or just being a good neighbour; whichever it was, she didn't hesitate to accept. As Eoin had predicted it turned out to be a most enjoyable night. Lisa loved listening to the Irish music and chatting to the locals; she couldn't believe how friendly everyone was towards her. The best part of the night, however, was when they came back to the house. She thought she was dreaming when Eoin kissed her and asked if she'd go out with him again. And that was the beginning of their romance.

In the weeks and months that followed Lisa had a lot to think about. She knew that meeting Eoin was the best thing that ever happened to her. In all the years she had been going out with William she never felt the same way about him as she felt about Eoin although she'd only known him for a short time. Her head was telling her one thing but her heart was telling her another. Surely, the sensible thing to do would be to sell the property, go back to New York, marry William and get on with her life. At least he'd be happy and so would her mother. But what about her and Eoin? She knew she'd never be happy without him, even if it meant giving up a life of comfort in New York for an isolated farmhouse in the west of Ireland. It was a big decision but one she'd have to make very soon.

Being an organised sort and wanting to keep busy, Lisa spent part of each day cleaning and tidying the house. She started with the kitchen and then moved on to the sitting-room. Gathering up any old rubbish which was lying around she carried it down to the lower end of the yard and placed it in a barrel to be burned. When she had the downstairs rooms sorted out, it was time to start on the bedrooms upstairs. Pulling out a drawer, to see if it contained anything for the rubbish heap, she was surprised to find a sealed envelope with her name written on it in pen. Wondering what it contained she sat down on the bed and tore it open.

>*Dear Lisa,*
>
>*I'm sorry we never met in person but happy that you have arrived in Ireland. Your grandfather, James, and I were very close growing up and when he emigrated to America I was heart-broken. I always hoped he'd return someday, but of course he never did. I know you have your own life in New York and it would be a huge step to take, but it would make me very happy to think that you might come back to live in the house where your grandfather and I grew up together. However, I will not try to influence you one way or the other. The only advice I can give you is to follow your heart and everything else will fall into place.*
>
>*Your Grandaunt, Elizabeth*

When she had finished reading, Lisa sat

there thinking about the contents of the letter. Although she had been living in her grandaunt's house for some time, it was only now she felt a real connection, almost as if she had actually known her. But that wasn't all: her grandaunt had said the only advice she could give her was to follow her heart, and that was precisely what she would do. Lisa knew now she was here to stay, and she couldn't wait to share the good news with Eoin.

THE FIRST COMMUNION PRESENT

If Joey's fairy godmother suddenly appeared to him and told him he could have one wish, he knew exactly what he would ask for: a spin on the back of his father's motorbike. Every evening at a quarter to five he'd stand at the gate waiting for his father to come home from work. As soon as he arrived he put the bike into the little shed at the side of the house. Sometimes on a Saturday or Sunday he'd take it out for a spin, but no matter how much Joey begged and pleaded with him he'd never take him.

Joey was a five year old boy who lived with his parents, Jenny and Paul, and two older sisters, in a large housing estate on the outskirts of town. His parents had married very young. Paul had always been a bit of a tearaway who was fond of spending his time and money with the lads in the local pubs. After his marriage he surprised everyone, however, by the way he settled down and took on his responsibilities. Instead of going out every night he now only had a couple of drinks at the week-end.

The family were doing alright as Paul had a good job in a large manufacturing company in the town. They weren't, by any means, well off but had enough to pay the rent and get by from week to week. Then out of the blue disaster struck. One Monday morning, when they turned up for work as usual, the workers received the shocking news that the company was closing down. They were given one month's notice, and that was it. Along with all the other workers Paul was devastated. It was the early nineteen eighties and unemployment was high so he'd have very little chance of getting another job.

When he broke the news to Jenny she was

equally upset. Having been used to her husband bringing home a decent weekly wage, how was she supposed to manage on a social welfare allowance? It was unthinkable. So a week later, when Paul announced that he was thinking of going to find work in England, she didn't object. She knew they would all miss him, but to her way of thinking, the money was more important. What was the use of a man who moped around the house all week and queued for the dole on a Thursday, when he could be beyond in England earning good money and sending it home to her and the children?

And so, when Paul had worked out his notice at the factory he packed his bags and headed off to England. Joey was heartbroken as he watched his father put the motorbike in the shed for the last time; now he might never get that spin that he had always longed for. Before he left, Paul promised he'd be home again to see them all in a few months, and then he was on his way.

Paul wasn't long in England when he secured a job on a building site. The pay was far better than what he had been earning in Ireland and, as he had promised, at the end of each month he sent home a cheque to his wife. Jenny was very pleased with how things were working out now. Not only had she sufficient money to run the house, but she also managed to put away a little for a rainy day. Jenny was a proud woman who always liked to keep up with the Joneses. When the children went back to school in September she made sure they were kitted out with new clothes and shoes; she couldn't bear the thought of her children being looked down upon or ridiculed by those who were better off. And then there were special occasions such as First Communions to think about. It wasn't just the child receiving the sacrament who had to be fitted out for that day, but the whole family had to look decent and respectable as well.

Now that there was enough money to cover expenses, however, the only problem was that the "whole family" was never together to celebrate these special occasions. It was two years since Paul had emigrated and it all that time he had never been home for a visit. While they would all like to see him, the one who missed him most was Joey. Not a day went by that he didn't think about him, and every night before he went to bed he looked in through the little window in the shed to make sure the motorbike was still there; somehow it helped him to feel closer to his father.

It was the month of March and Joey, who was now seven years old, was to receive his First Holy Communion in June. His class had been practicing all year for the big day, but now that there were only three months left, the preparations were really getting into full swing. There was Catechism to be learned, dresses and suits to be bought, and family gatherings to be organised. However, in spite of all the excitement going on around him, there was only one question on Joey's mind: would his father come home for his big day? He'd been gone two years and Joey couldn't wait to see him again. So, when his mother wrote a letter to Paul telling him the date of the First Communion and asking him to come home for it, Joey was delighted; he was sure his father wouldn't let him down.

One day in school the master informed the class that the parish priest was coming to check how the First Communion preparations were going. He warned them all to brush up on their Catechism and be on their best behaviour on the day. The following Friday morning at 10'oclock the priest arrived. He took a seat at the top of the classroom beside the master and the two chatted for a few minutes. Then he turned to the children and cleared his throat.

"Now, just a few questions to see if you are all fit to receive the sacraments," he announced in his official voice.

The children were petrified. What if they didn't know the answers to the questions? Would they still get their First Communion? However, once things got started it wasn't as bad as they had expected. The priest moved around the room randomly asking questions here and there. They weren't too difficult and most of the pupils were getting them right. Eventually, he came to Joey.

"Now Joey, I have a question for you and I want you to think very carefully because there's only one right answer. What are you looking forward to most on your First Communion Day?"

Joey's face lit up with delight. The priest couldn't have asked him an easier question. He definitely knew the answer to this one.

"I'm looking forward to my father coming home from England and bringing me for a spin on the back of his motorbike."

To Joey's utter dismay the priest looked shocked, and after glancing at the master he shook his head sadly. Little Mary, who was the teacher's pet and could always be depended upon to have the correct answer, put up her hand.

"Well Mary, what are *you* most looking forward to on First Communion Day?" "Please father," answered Mary, in her most angelic voice, "I'm looking forward to receiving the host, which is really the body and blood of Christ, for the first time." "Excellent Mary," said the priest, as he handed her a lovely, new, shiny sixpence.

After he had asked a few more questions the priest seemed satisfied that in general the children were receiving adequate preparation for their First Communion and to their absolute delight he gave them the rest of the day off. The following Monday, however, when Joey went into school he had to face the wrath of the schoolmaster. He was told he had let down the whole class by giving the priest such a ridiculous answer to his question; how could he be so stupid?

"I wouldn't mind if it was true" continued the master in front of the whole class, "but your father probably won't even bother to come home. He didn't come home when your sister made her First Communion, so why should he come for yours?"

Joey was mortified. He had never felt more like crying, but somehow he managed to hold back the tears. He hated the master for the way he had spoken about his father; just wait, he thought, until the tenth of June and then we'll see who's right. However, a week later Joey received another setback. He went home from school one evening to find that a letter from his father had arrived saying that he wouldn't be able to come home for the First Communion. He explained that his boss wouldn't allow him to take time off, June being the busiest month of year on the building sites. Of course, this was just an excuse.

Ever since Paul had gone to England he had fallen back into some of the bad old habits of his younger days. The trouble was, now that he had a good job and was far away from home, he had too much money and time on his hands. Although he always managed to send home the cheque to his family, any spare cash he had left over was spent in the pub. He sometimes thought he should save up to go home for a holiday, but time slipped by and he never got around to it. So the real reason he wouldn't be coming home was he simply wouldn't have the money to do so.

Joey was very upset when he heard the bad news. He begged his mother to write again to his father to try to persuade him to change his mind, but she said there was no point; he had made it clear he wouldn't be coming and Joey would just have to make the best of it. However, Joey couldn't give up on his dream just like that; there must be some way, he thought, to get his father to come home. The following evening on the way home from school he told his best friend, Danny, about his dilemma. Danny thought for a moment.

"Why don't you write to your father yourself and tell him how important it is for him to come home?"

Joey was taken aback; he knew nothing about writing letters. "How would I write to him? Sure I don't know his address."

"Well, you'll just have to find his address, won't you?" replied Danny. "Your mother probably keeps his letters in her room. All you have to do is find one and copy down the address. Then you can write to him. It's as simple as that."

That night when his mother was busy in the kitchen Joey sneaked into her bedroom, found one of the letters from his father and put it in his pocket. When he went to bed he copied the address from the top of the page onto a piece of paper. The following night he repeated the exercise, this time returning the letter to where he found it. Thankfully, his mother hadn't noticed it missing. The next night when he went to bed Joey wrote the letter. His handwriting wasn't great but he did his best. He told his father how much he missed him and begged him to come home for his First Communion Day. After several false starts he finally completed the letter and got it posted. Now all he had to do was wait and hope.

On the morning of the First Communion everyone was up early. Of course Joey was the centre of attention. His mother helped him to put on the brand new suit she had bought him and laced up his new black shiny shoes. When she was finished with him he looked like a new pin. Joey, however, had other things on his mind. Although he hadn't heard a word from his father since he sent the letter, and it was now the day of the First Communion and there was no sign of him, he still wouldn't give up hope. Maybe he got delayed and he'll just go straight to the church, he thought. However, when they arrived at the church and there was still no sign of him anywhere Joey began to feel worried; perhaps he wasn't coming after all. As he took his place with all the other children at the front of the church he knew this was supposed to be the happiest day of his life, but all he could feel was an overwhelming sense of disappointment. However, he knew his mother would be watching his every move, so he pulled himself together and tried to pretend that everything was ok.

When the ceremony was over the children all marched down the aisle, two by two, and out into the yard where they were quickly surrounded by the other members of the family. Joey was joined by, not only his mother and sisters, but also aunts, uncles and several cousins who had been invited to take part in the celebrations. They had all gathered into a group, and the photographer was just about to take the family picture, when suddenly, Joey spotted his father making his way across the churchyard. Forgetting all about the photograph, he broke away from the group and ran across to meet him shouting "Daddy, Daddy, I knew you'd come!" His father gave him a huge hug and then both of them took their place for the all-important family photo.

An hour later they were all back at the house tucking into the feast Jenny had prepared for them.

"What are you planning on doing for the afternoon?" Joey's mother asked him.

"Oh I don't know, I suppose we'll play a few games of football," replied Joey.

"Sounds like a good idea," said his father, "but there's something you and I have to do first, Joey."

"What?"

"How about going for that spin on the motorbike you always wanted?"

"Yes!!!"

Reaching over and picking up big slice of his mother's delicious Victoria sponge, Joey thought that perhaps these First Communion days weren't so bad after all.

THE GOLD PENDANT

It was a warm sunny day in the month of June, nineteen fifty-one. Peter Donovan was ravenous as he'd been in the field since eight that morning. Returning to the house at one o'clock he hoped the dinner would be on the table, and he wasn't disappointed. His wife, Annie, who was a great cook, had everything ready. As soon as he came into the kitchen she dished out the bacon and cabbage and placed a large bowl of steaming hot potatoes in the centre of the table.

"Where are the children?" he asked, as he took a large potato from the bowl and started to peel it.

"They're across the road playing in that trickle of water they call the river. I'll go and get them."

A few minutes later she came back into the kitchen followed by the two children. The eldest was a four year old boy called James, and his younger sister, Kate, was almost three. Taking them over to the small sink in the corner she gave their hands and faces a quick rub of a cloth, and it wasn't long until they were all seated around the table tucking into the hearty meal.

When they were finished Peter went back to the field and Annie washed the dishes and tidied up the kitchen. The children hung around for a little while, but they soon got bored and went back across the road to play in the water. It was only a tiny stream which flowed past their house on the opposite side of the road but they loved it; to them it was like having their very own river. They'd make little boats out of paper or bits of sticks and watch them float about. Although they weren't short of toys to play with, messing about in the water was their favourite game.

Sometimes when they came in all wet and mucky their mother wished they could play at something cleaner. However, apart from the mess she didn't really mind as she could keep an eye on them from the kitchen window and she always knew they were safe.

At the back of the house Annie kept a little garden where she grew all sorts of vegetables and herbs for the kitchen. When she was finished the washing-up she went out to the garden to get some fresh lettuce, as she was planning to make a nice salad for the tea that evening. While there she spent some time pulling up weeds which she thought always seemed to grow faster than anything else in the garden. She was so engrossed in what she was doing that almost half an hour passed by without her realising it. When she returned to the kitchen and looked out through the window she could see Jack, but there was no sign of Kate. She went out and hurried across the road.

"Where's Kate?"

"I don't know."

"What do you mean, you don't know? She

was here with you when I was going out to the garden."

"She must have gone into the house when I wasn't looking."

Annie ran back to the house calling her daughter at the top of her voice but got no reply. When she had checked all the rooms, she went back out to the yard again and continued calling her name. She was beginning to panic now. Where could she be? She went back and questioned James again but he wasn't able to provide her with any more information. Their nearest neighbour, old Lizzie Murphy, who lived in a small cottage next door, stayed with James while Annie went to break the news to Peter.

What had started off as an ordinary summer day for the Donovan family had suddenly turned in to the worst nightmare imaginable. Peter hurried to the big farmer's house down the road and telephoned the guards. They soon arrived at the house and questioned everybody about the events of the afternoon. Annie gave them a detailed description of Kate and the clothes she was wearing; she even remembered to mention the small gold necklace which had been given to her by her godmother on her christening day and was supposed to be a lucky charm. Annie wondered now if it would live up to its name and help to bring her daughter back home.

James had told his mother earlier that he hadn't seen anybody passing by, however when the guards questioned him he suddenly remembered that he'd seen a caravan of gypsies. When the guards heard this they were immediately suspicious and set off, with James and his father, in pursuit. About five miles away they came to a halting site where James pointed out the caravan he'd seen earlier in the day. A thin, shifty-looking man of about forty with long, greasy hair came out to speak to the guards. They informed him they were looking for a three year old child who was missing from her home.

"And what's that got to do with me?" he asked with a sneer.

"We're just wondering if you saw her on the road today during your travels. Your caravan was seen passing by her home around the time she went missing," replied the guard. "Are you suggesting I had something to do with her disappearance? I'll tell you something guard, I have six little darlins of my own in that caravan, and if I could get someone to take a few of them off my hands I'd be a happy man."

"You won't mind then if we have a look inside."

The guards carried out a thorough search of the caravan but, unfortunately, there was no trace of little Kate. After that the search continued in the area for weeks, with notices being displayed in the newspapers and on the radio, but with no success. Both the guards and the family were still suspicious that the gypsies were in some way involved but, unfortunately, they could find no proof. As time went by hope of finding her began to fade and eventually the search was called off. The family were heartbroken at the loss of their little girl but somehow life had to go on. They had to think of their other child, James, as well. A year after Kate went missing they had another baby girl whom they called

Eileen. The baby gave them a new lease of life, but they never gave up hope that someday they'd see their beloved Kate again.

The years passed and it was now September, nineteen seventy. Nothing had changed much for Annie and Peter. They were still making a living on the little farm. James who was now twenty-three had got a good job in a factory in the town. He helped out at home when things were busy but had no real interest in becoming a full time farmer. Eileen who had just turned eighteen had grown up to be a good-looking girl with long black hair and blue eyes. Having obtained excellent results in her Leaving Certificate examination, she had just recently been offered a job in the civil service in Dublin where she was to start work in a couple of weeks.

In spite of the events which had taken place before she was born, Eileen had a relatively happy childhood. Although she grew up with the knowledge that she had an older sister who had mysteriously disappeared, it was obvious that her parents or brother didn't want to talk about what had happened, so she never asked. There were no photographs of her around the house either, as in those days most country people didn't have a camera to take family photos.

Eileen was excited about starting her new life in Dublin. At first she stayed in a hostel run by nuns which catered for young girls from the country who were starting out in their first job. It wasn't long until she teamed up with two others who were in the same boat as herself, and they rented their first flat together. For a while everything felt new and strange to her. She could hardly wait for Friday evening to come when she could get the bus home. However, as time passed she settled in. She got on well with her flatmates and they became the best of friends. There was so much to do in the city they were never bored. During the week they'd often go to the cinema or theatre, but when the weekend came round they'd go dancing in the National Ballroom in Parnell Square; if you were a culchie in Dublin in the nineteen seventies that was the place to be! From then on the trips home were reduced to once a month.

Although Annie did her best to hide her feelings, she missed Eileen terribly when she went to work in Dublin. She was glad, of course, that her daughter was now an independent young woman making her own way in the world, but that didn't stop her from feeling lonely. She still had her husband and son at home, but it wasn't the same. Every time her daughter returned to Dublin Annie waved her off with a smile on her face even though she felt as if her heart was breaking. She also found herself thinking more about her other daughter, Kate, whom she had lost all those years ago. Annie had always been convinced that the child had been stolen by the gypsies that day and given, probably in exchange for money, to some couple who were desperate for a child. She hoped that, wherever she was, life had been good to her. If she had one wish it would be to see her daughter again so that she could know for certain that everything had turned out well for her, but that was highly unlikely.

One weekend towards the end of

November, Eileen made her usual visit home to see her parents. They were all sitting around the table tucking into the Sunday roast when suddenly she had an idea.

"Mam, why don't you come up to Dublin on the 8th of December for the big culchie shopping day?"
"Oh, I don't know Eileen," replied her mother, laughing, "sure I wouldn't have a clue how to get around Dublin, I'd probably end up getting lost."

Now that Eileen had got the idea into her head, she really wanted her mother to come to Dublin for the day. She'd enjoy nothing better than taking her around the shops and helping her to pick out a few bits and pieces for the Christmas festivities. Eventually, after much persuasion she agreed to go. Eileen gave her strict instructions: she was to get off the bus at O'Connell Bridge, go into the cafe beside the bus stop, buy herself a cup of tea and wait there until Eileen arrived.

The 8th of December came round and everything was going as planned. Annie followed her daughter's instructions to the letter, and by eleven o'clock she was sitting comfortably in the little cafe with a nice cup of tea and a hot buttered scone on the table in front of her. She was glad she had made it this far without any hitches. She could relax now and enjoy her cuppa, and hopefully, her daughter would arrive by the time she was finished. As she sat there sipping her tea she idly looked around at the other customers. At the next table to hers she noticed a young couple with a little girl about two years old. The woman had long blond hair, the man was dark and handsome and all three were very well dressed.

Annie was concentrating on buttering her scone when suddenly the little girl got down from her chair, as children often do in cafes when they get bored, and wandered over to Annie's table. She was a beautiful child with dark curly hair. They smiled at each other and Annie said hello and asked what her name was. She didn't answer but just kept on smiling. It was then that she noticed it! On a gold chain around the child's neck hung a tiny pendant in the centre of which was a blue

Forget Me Not flower; it was exactly the same as the necklace her daughter was wearing on the day she went missing. She just sat there staring at it for what seemed like an eternity but was, in reality, just a few seconds. Then there was a movement at the next table. The young woman got up from her seat and approached Annie's table holding out her hand to the child.

"Come along now Deirdre," she said smiling "and don't be annoying the lady."
"She's not annoying me at all," replied Annie, "I was actually enjoying our little chat. I hope you don't mind me saying, but that's a beautiful pendant she's wearing."
"Oh thanks, that belonged to me when I was a baby, according to my mother it was some sort of family heirloom."

Just before the young woman turned away Annie looked into her eyes, and at that moment she knew without any shadow of a doubt that she was looking at none other than her own daughter. A few seconds later she watched as the trio walked out the door onto the busy sidewalk where they were swallowed up by the passing crowd. Annie sat there feeling like somebody in a trance. Had that really happened or did she just imagine it? Then she remembered that Eileen would be arriving any minute, so she pulled herself together as best she could.

Annie never told anybody about the strange experience she had in Dublin that day; she didn't think anyone would believe her. More than likely, she would never see her daughter again, but knowing that she had a good life and seemed to be happy brought her great peace of mind. After all, what more could any mother wish for?

A TERRIBLE SECRET

On a chilly March evening Maggie washed the dishes and tidied up the kitchen as she had done every evening for as long as she could remember. When she was finished she went into the sitting-room, turned up the television, and flopped down in her comfortable old armchair beside the fire. Ah, peace at last, she thought. Her favourite soap was just starting and if she was lucky she might get half an hour to watch it without interruption. However, it was not to be; five minutes later she heard the faint tap, tap, tap, of her father's walking stick coming from the bedroom upstairs. With a sigh, Maggie got to her feet, turned down the television and made for the stairs.

Edward Carey was ninety-six years old and Maggie was his full-time carer. During the past few weeks she had noticed his health deteriorating; in fact, she didn't think he had long left. They lived in a sturdy two-story house in the rural townland of Kilrane. When Maggie was a child there was a pub attached to the dwelling which was frequented mainly by locals. Maggie's father, Edward, who also had a small farm, ran the pub himself as had his father and grandfather before him. A handful of men would gather for a drink and a chat at night; women were rarely seen in a pub in those days.

Maggie, who was an only child, was born in nineteen-fifty. When she was growing up her father never had much time for her, although he was quick enough to chastise her if she misbehaved. The truth was, he was disappointed that he didn't have a son to carry on the business and farm after his day. Maggie more or less kept out of his way as much as she could and, of course, she was never allowed anywhere near the pub at any time of the day or night. Despite this Maggie had been a happy child. She had a good relationship with her mother, Kathleen, and when she started attending the local school she made lots of friends her own age. Then on a cold December night when she was ten years old she witnessed an incident which changed everything.

Although her parents never let her go into the pub, Maggie had devised her own means of watching events from a distance. There were three rooms upstairs. Her parents' bedroom was over the kitchen, Maggie's was over the sitting-room and the third was a spare room which was over the pub. A long time ago she had discovered a small crack in the ceiling of the spare room which she had never told anyone about. When she got bored in her own room she'd often sneak next door, remove a piece of old lino which covered the hole, and lying there on her stomach in the dark, she could hear and see practically everything that went on in the pub below.

On this particular night in early December,

Maggie went up to her bedroom at about eight o'clock to begin her homework. A couple of hours later when she was finished she decided to go next door and see what was happening down below. Her mother was tidying up behind the bar. Her father and three other men were playing cards with their pints on the table in front of them. Two of the men were young, in their twenties or early thirties, she thought, and the third was older, probably in his fifties. Maggie had seen them all before as they were regulars, but she didn't know their names. There was nobody else in the pub. As she watched everything was quiet for a while until suddenly the two younger men started arguing. She couldn't hear what they were saying, but it seemed like one of them was accusing the other of cheating. As the minutes went by they were getting angrier, and before long they were both on their feet throwing punches at each other.

Maggie was fascinated by the scene unfolding before her eyes; she had never seen anything like this before. Her mother was shouting at them to stop, her father and the other man were trying to scramble out of the way, and the two lads were punching each other as if they were competing for a world title. Then things took a turn for the worse. One of the combatants hit the other a particularly hard blow which caused him to stumble and fall backwards. He went flying through the air and a loud crack could be heard as his head came in contact with the stone fireplace. Maggie watched in horror as the young man slumped to the ground where he lay motionless, his face as white as a sheet.

From then on it seemed as if everything was happening in slow motion. Although Maggie was shaking with terror, she couldn't drag her eyes away from the scene below her. For a few moments, the four people stood staring in silence at the man on the floor. When they did start talking they spoke to each other in whispers, so Maggie couldn't hear what they were saying. Her mother knelt down beside the young man, felt his pulse and then shook her head. After that they all continued talking in whispers for some time. Eventually, her mother and father left the room and came back a few minutes later carrying a piece of old carpet. They spread the carpet on the floor, lifted the man onto it and rolled him up in it. It was only then the terrible truth dawned on her; he was dead! She watched in horror as the three men carried the bundle from the room while her mother ran in front of them to open the door.

Maggie was shaking as she got up from her position on the floor and made her way back to her own room. She somehow managed to put on her nightdress and got into bed pulling the blankets over her head. As she lay there shivering all she could think about was where they were going to take the dead man. Eventually, curiosity got the better of her so she got out of bed again and went over to the window. When she looked out she got another shock. About fifty yards from the house, where there was a piece of disused ground, she could see a flickering light and when she opened the window she could hear the sound of someone shoveling clay. Her worst fears were realised; they were burying the body. Closing the window she got back into bed. As she lay there in the darkness she kept telling herself that it was all a nightmare from which she had just woken up, until eventually she managed to fall asleep.

When she woke to the sound of her mother's voice calling her for school in the morning, her first thought was that it was just an ordinary day, but then it all came flooding back, the terrible events she had witnessed the night before. Was everything going to be different, she wondered, or would life go on as usual. She decided the best thing she could do was to try to carry on as normal and see what would happen.

When she went down to the kitchen she was relieved to find it the same as any other morning. Her father was sitting in his usual place at the table, and her mother was busy preparing the breakfast. Her father said little, but there was nothing unusual about that; Edward Carey was never in a good mood early in the morning, especially if he was after having a few too many the night before, which was often the case. Despite the drawn, worried look on her mother's face she carried on as usual. She asked Maggie if she had slept well and then served up the usual breakfast of porridge, tea and toast. When she had finished eating, Maggie put her lunch box into her schoolbag and, saying good-bye to her parents, hurried off to school.

During the day she tried her best to act normal, but Maggie found it difficult to concentrate on her lessons. The teacher asked her several times if there was something wrong, but she assured her she was ok. When she got home that evening she found that nothing had changed. After a few days she began to realise that this was how things were going to be; nobody was going to own up to what had happened. Even when she heard in school a few days later that a local man, Sean Murray, was missing, she knew his death wasn't going to be revealed by those responsible, and she would have to keep her terrible secret.

For several weeks after that the police carried out an investigation into the disappearance of Sean Murray, and it was the main topic on everyone's lips. However, no trace of the missing man was found, and slowly life went back to normal, and the incident faded into the background. The Carey family also carried on as if nothing had happened. The only thing that changed was a couple of weeks later her father announced he was closing the pub. His customers tried to talk him out of it, but he told them he wasn't making any profit and he'd decided to concentrate his energy on the farm instead.

Although time passed and life went on around her, things were never the same again for Maggie, as she was forever haunted by the awful scenes she witnessed that night. Terrified that she might let something slip, she no longer confided in anyone and became something of a loner. When she left school she didn't go out to work like other young girls but stayed at home with her parents helping out in the house and on the farm. When her mother became ill she looked after her until she passed away. Now, sixty years later, she was still looking after her father who, apart from herself, was the only remaining survivor of that terrible night.

Maggie had often wondered if her father would confess everything before he died; or would he take his secret with him to the grave?

When she went up the stairs on that chilly March evening and entered his bedroom, Maggie's father was sitting up in the bed looking frail but anxious.

"What's wrong Father?" she asked, "you look upset."

"Will you get the priest for me, Maggie? I want to make my confession."

"Of course Father, is there anything else you want me to do?"

"Yes, while you're at it, will you call the guards as well?"

"The guards?" Maggie tried to sound surprised.

"Yes, the guards. They need to hear what I have to say as well."

"Alright Father, I'll call them first thing in the morning"

"No Maggie, call them now; I might not be here in the morning."

Maggie phoned Fr. O'Keeffe and Sergeant

Moran and, after explaining the situation, both of them agreed to call out to the house that night. Fr. O'Keeffe was first to arrive and Maggie brought him into the sitting room to await the sergeant's arrival. When half an hour had passed and they were beginning to think he wasn't coming, Sergeant Moran arrived and they all went up to Edward's room. He was lying back on the pillows with his eyes closed. Maggie shook him gently, "Wake up Father, Sergeant Moran and Fr. O'Keeffe are here." There was no response. She tried again, but still nothing. Fr. O'Keeffe went over and felt his pulse. "I'm sorry Maggie," he said, "your father has passed away"

After Fr. O'Keeffe had performed the last rights and no more could be done for her father, Maggie took the two men back downstairs and into the sitting room. There she produced a bottle of whiskey, poured them a glass each and one for herself. She thanked them both for coming out at such a late hour and Fr. O'Keeffe for performing the last rites.

"I wonder what he was going to confess,"

said Sergeant Moran, as he gazed into the dying embers of the fire, "It must have been serious, but I suppose we'll never know now."

This was the moment Maggie had been waiting for. She told them the whole story from beginning to end, without adding or leaving out anything. When she was finished they were staring at her in astonishment.

"That must have been a heavy burden to carry for all those years," said Fr. O'Keeffe, "why did you never tell anyone before now?"

"I always felt it wasn't my place to get involved, so I tried to put it to the back of my mind, but it wasn't easy. By the way, Sergeant," she asked as she took a sip from her glass, "will I be in trouble for not reporting a crime?"

"I wouldn't think so, Maggie. You were a ten year old child who witnessed something she should never have seen. I think you've probably suffered enough keeping it to yourself all these years. You deserve a bit of peace for the rest of your days."

Three months later Maggie was relaxing on the old wooden bench in her little garden. She was all alone in the world now, but that didn't bother her; all she felt was a wonderful sense of peace. Now that everything was out in the open, she was determined to enjoy the remainder of her days and she swore she'd never keep a secret again as long as she lived.

A CHANGE OF HEART

Jamie Johnston was a fourteen year old boy who had an extremely negative attitude to life. He hated his home in a dilapidated block of flats near the centre of town. He was in first year in the local secondary school, and he hated that too. Jamie had never been interested in sports or any other extracurricular activities so he had very few friends; in fact, he was generally regarded as a bit of a loner. He was the youngest child in a family of six. His parents were a decent, hard-working couple who had reared their children as best they could. The two eldest were now married, two more were working in Dublin and the fifth, who was nineteen, was away in college. You might think that being the only one living at home and having his parents all to himself would have made Jamie happy, but it didn't.

To make matters worse he wasn't doing well in school either. He had no interest in any of the subjects being taught, and he was regarded as one of the biggest troublemakers in the school. Eventually, the teachers gave up on him. If they could manage to keep him under control at all they were happy enough; as far as teaching him anything went, it was out of the question.

It was now the year two thousand and five, and computers and information technology were the "in" thing. A computer lab had recently been set up in the school Jamie attended. Although information technology still wasn't a school subject, computer workshops were held once a week for all students. At first, Jamie was as sceptical about these classes as he was about everything else, but it wasn't long until he began to take an interest in them. The teacher was amazed at how fast he could pick up the new skills and soon he appeared to know more than the teacher himself.

Now that Jamie had found this new interest he wished he could get a laptop of his own. However, when he asked his parents to buy him one, they said it was out of the question. They just couldn't afford it; he'd have to wait until he was older. He was disappointed, but not the least bit surprised. It was the same old story; if it had been one of his siblings they wouldn't have been refused, but he never got anything he asked for. Life was so unfair! Still he wasn't about to give up; he'd just have to think of some other way to get the money.

Over the days and weeks which followed Jamie racked his brains trying to think of a way to get enough money to buy a laptop. The thought occurred to him that he might be able to get a part-time job for the week-ends, however, on approaching several shops and small businesses in the area, no luck. They all had the same story: at fourteen he was too young to be covered by insurance. Nobody would take him on until he was at least sixteen. So, what was he to do? Wait for two whole years before he could get his hands on some money? No, he'd have to think of something else.

One Friday morning during the Easter school holidays Jamie's mother sent him down to the post office to post a letter for her. After much grumbling and complaining and wanting to know why she couldn't do it herself, he took the letter and the money, got up on his bicycle and pedalled off towards the post office. He thought he'd only be a few minutes, but when he arrived there were several people there before him, so he had to join the queue. As he stood there he wondered why there were so many people in the post office that morning; surely it couldn't be this busy all the time. Then he noticed that all the people before and behind him in the queue were elderly, and suddenly it struck him; they must be there to collect the old age pension. Just my luck, thought Jamie impatiently, now I'm stuck here for the rest of the day!

After that the queue moved along at a

snail's pace as each of the pensioners approached the counter, greeted the clerk, and handed in their pension book. Then they had to wait for the money to be dispensed, check to make sure it was all there, stash it away in a wallet or handbag, bid goodbye to the clerk and slowly move away to make room for the next customer. Finally, after what seemed like an eternity, it was almost Jamie's turn. He watched as the old man in front of him hobbled up to the counter with the aid of his walking stick, collected his pension and carefully deposited it in the inside pocket of his overcoat before leaving the post office. "Next Please!" Jamie hurried up to the counter to buy his stamp.

A few minutes later Jamie was cycling back up the road towards home when he spotted the elderly gentleman, who had been before him in the queue, making his way slowly along the footpath in the same direction as himself. Almost without realising what he was doing, and instead of passing him by as he should have done, he slowed down and got off the bike. He was now walking about twenty yards behind the old man. I'm not in any hurry home, he thought, so I'll just stay behind him and see where he lives. Surely there's no law against that! After about ten minutes the old man came to his house, went in and closed the door behind him. The only thought in Jamie's mind at that moment was here was his chance to get the money he needed to buy the computer. Getting up on his bicycle he cycled around the block a few times to clear his head and formulate a plan of action. Then he went boldly up to the old man's door and knocked. The door opened slowly.

"Hello, how can I help you?"
"I'm sorry to bother you sir, but my dog has gone missing and I was just wondering if you had seen him around."
"Oh, I'm sorry to hear that. What type of dog is he?"
"He's a small black and white Jack Russell with a brown collar."
"No, I'm afraid I haven't seen him but I will certainly keep an eye out for him. Come in to the kitchen and you can give me your address and phone number."

Jamie was delighted. So far so good, he thought, as he followed him into the kitchen and looked around. It wasn't long until he spotted what he was looking for: a wallet which was lying on a shelf near the door. When the old man went into another room to look for a pen and paper, Jamie grabbed the wallet, ran out the door, jumped onto his bicycle and pedalled furiously away.

Later that evening in his bedroom he counted the money and felt sure he had enough to buy the laptop he so badly wanted. As he lay on his bed thinking about the amazing stroke of luck that had come his way he heard the doorbell ring. A few moments later his mother called him and when he went down the stairs his heart almost stopped when he saw two gardaí standing in the hallway. It turned out that old Mr. O'Reilly's neighbour, Mrs. Fitzpatrick, who was known to be a one-woman "neighbourhood watch", had seen the whole incident from her kitchen window. She recognised Jamie and called the gardaí without delay.

The money was promptly returned to its

rightful owner, but that wasn't the end of the matter for Jamie. He had to appear before the next sitting of the juvenile court where the judge handed down a community service order in lieu of detention. Both Jamie and his parents were relieved when they heard this; at least he wouldn't be sent away from home. They expected he'd be required to work with the local tidy towns group planting flowers and cutting grass, or perhaps painting and decorating a public building. However, two weeks later he found out what his actual community service was to be.

The local senior citizens group, who met every Tuesday afternoon in the community centre, had recently been presented with a set of laptops by a local businessman. All they needed now was somebody to teach them how to use them. So, when Jamie's liaison officer consulted with his teachers over what type of community service would be suitable for him, it all suddenly fell into place; the senior citizens needed a tutor and Jamie needed the work. It was arranged that for the next three months he would go every Tuesday to the community centre at four o'clock to teach the senior citizens how to use the laptops. Jamie was shocked when they told him what he would have to do.

"This must be a joke," he said to his parents, "sure what do I know about teaching computer classes to senior citizens?"
"Don't worry," replied his mother, "it won't take you long to get used to it. Your teachers say you're a whizz-kid on the computer. All you need is to have a bit of patience and I'm sure everything will work out fine."

Jamie wasn't so sure that things were going to work out, however, all he could do was give it his best shot. The first couple of classes were difficult for both the tutor and the learners and progress was slow. However, once they got the hang of it, the senior citizens turned out to be excellent students and it wasn't long until they were all googling away like true professionals. At the end of class one day, after they had mastered all the basics, Jamie announced that the following week he was going to show them how to use Skype. They all looked at him suspiciously.

Skipe, what was that, they wondered. Then Bridie Murphy, who had appointed herself a sort of spokeswoman for the group, spoke up:

"What in the name of God is a *skipe*? I don't like the sound of that at all, so I don't."

Jamie explained that Skype was simply a method of communicating with people where you could both speak to and see them at the same time. See the person at the other end of the line? There was no way that could possibly happen they thought, however, they were willing to give it a go anyway. The following week or two were spent practicing and soon they were able to contact their relatives not just in Ireland but as far away as America, Australia and New Zealand. This was amazing; a whole new world was opening up before their very eyes and they had Jamie to thank for it all.

Both Jamie and his students were sad when the three months of tuition came to an end. Now that the senior citizens had learned a little about the wonders of the internet, they felt their lives would never be dull again. Some of them were even making enquiries about getting their own computers. It wasn't just the senior citizens, however, who felt they had benefited from the course; the person who seemed to have gained the most of all was Jamie. His attitude to life had changed so much over the three months that he was almost like a different person. Even when the official classes came to an end Jamie still continued to visit the senior citizens once a month to see how they were progressing and help with any difficulties they might have.

A few years later when he had completed his secondary education nobody was surprised when Jamie went on to study computer science in college. Having graduated with a first class honours degree he eventually ended up working in one of the top positions in the Google head office in California. One Tuesday morning his secretary informed him that his presence was requested at an important meeting which was to take place at four o'clock that afternoon. He said he was terribly sorry but, as he had a prior engagement at that time, the meeting would have to be rescheduled.

At exactly four o'clock Jamie clicked on the Skype icon on his computer and a few seconds later a group of smiling senior citizens, sitting around a table, appeared on the screen. No matter how high his position in the company, or where in the world he was, Jamie never forgot his monthly check-in with the Senior Citizens Group in Ballymore. After all, as he often reminded himself, that was where it all began.

THE WHEELS OF LOVE

It was a warm evening towards the end of May with the hawthorn in full bloom. As eighteen year old Patricia walked down the road towards her home she was feeling both happy and sad at the same time. She was happy because in two weeks' time she'd be going to London to start her nurse's training and sad because she'd be leaving behind her home and family and everything she loved. Although she had always wanted to be a nurse, she had hoped she would be able to do her training in Ireland. However, getting a place in a hospital in Ireland in the nineteen-seventies was difficult so she and her parents decided the best option for her was to take the boat to England where thousands of Irish girls were nursing at that time.

It all started when at seven years old Patricia was involved in an accident which almost killed her. While helping to save the hay on her uncle's farm, she fell off the back of the tractor and the wheel of the trailer went over her. As a result, she had to spend three months in Crumlin Children's Hospital in Dublin. For Patricia that was the worst time of her life. She seldom received a visit from her parents. It wasn't that they didn't want to visit her, but circumstances made it difficult. It was the nineteen sixties, they lived at the other side of the country, and they didn't have a car. Once a month her mother would make the trip to Dublin and on those occasions she would only be able to spend a couple of hours with Patricia when she'd have to leave to catch the bus back home again.

When her mother left to go home Patricia would be inconsolable. No matter what the nurses did they couldn't get any good of her. She'd roar and bawl her head off for the rest of the evening until finally she'd cry herself to sleep. While all the nurses were kind to Patricia and the other children in the ward, there was one nurse called Mary who she remembered best of all. One morning, after her mother's visit and having cried herself to sleep the night before, Patricia woke up feeling miserable as usual. As she sat up and looked around she saw a mysterious looking bag on the end of her bed. Nurse Mary was on duty that morning and when she came over to her bed Patricia asked her what was in it.

"Why don't you open it and see for yourself?", smiled the nurse as she picked up the bag and handed it to her.

Patricia was almost afraid to open it, but curiosity got the better of her. Imagine her surprise when she put in her hand and pulled out a gorgeous doll about twelve inches in height with fair hair and dressed in a smart nurse's uniform. The best thing about it, though, was the eyes. They were a pale blue colour, and when she looked into them they seemed to tell her that everything was going to be alright. Patricia had never seen anything so beautiful before in her life.

Over the following weeks Nurse Mary was glad she'd given the doll to Patricia. It had been Mary's favourite doll when she was a child, but for years now it had been sitting on top of the wardrobe gathering dust. She was so glad that it had gone to a good home. It seemed to make such a difference to Patricia; she was like a different child. Instead of fretting she now spent all her time playing with her doll, and she seemed so much happier in herself. A few weeks later, when she was allowed to go home, Patricia brought the doll with her. She always kept it on the locker beside her bed and she swore that she would never part with it no matter what happened. It was shortly after her stay in hospital, too, that she announced she was going to be a nurse when she grew up. Her parents thought she'd forget about it over the years, but she never did.

The following week, as she prepared for her journey, Patricia made sure to pack her most treasured possession, the blue-eyed doll.

When she had everything ready she said goodbye to her family and friends and set off for London. Her mother had arranged with a cousin who lived in London to meet her and see her safely to the nurses' home which was to be her new abode. During her first week or two in London Patricia, naturally, felt homesick for her friends and family. However, it wasn't long until she got to know other girls who were in the same boat as herself, and when training started she was so busy that she hardly had time to think about anything else.

Once she had settled into her new surroundings and become accustomed to life in London the time flew by, and before she realised it Patricia was nearing the end of her three years training. The final month of her course was spent working on the paediatric ward. When that was finished all she'd have to do was her final exams, and then, with a bit of luck, she'd be a fully qualified nurse. Of all the different sections of the hospital she had been assigned to over the three years, the paediatric ward was the one she'd been looking forward to most. And she wasn't disappointed; she thoroughly enjoyed working with the children.

There was one little girl there, called Angie, who was five years old and was recovering from a serious illness. Her parents only came to see her occasionally as they were poor and lived a long way from the hospital. The nurses were extremely kind to her, but she never responded. She reminded Patricia of herself when she had been in hospital as a child, and how lonely and sad she had felt at that time. Knowing she wasn't supposed to get emotionally attached to her patients, Patricia still couldn't help wishing she could do something to cheer her up.

Then one night as she lay in bed thinking about the problem, she suddenly realised that there *was* something she could do. So, on her last day working on the children's ward Patricia brought her beloved doll in her bag, and while Angie was asleep, she tucked it in beside her in the bed. Before she left that evening she peeped into the ward again and saw Angie sitting up talking to the doll with a huge smile on her face. She hoped that Angie would one day remember the kindness she had received from the nurses, and she, in her turn, would pass it on to someone else; and the wheels of love go round…..

AN ACTIVE RETIREMENT

Jerome O'Shaughnessy woke at daybreak on a Friday morning in late June. As he lay there listening to the birds chirping in the trees which surrounded his little bungalow, he thought sadly, it's here at last: the day I've been dreading for so long. Jerome had been a teacher for over forty years and today was the day of his retirement. Maybe if I put my head under the blankets and refuse to get up, he thought, this nightmare will go away, and when Monday comes around I'll still be a teacher in Glenbawn National School. He knew, however, that this was just wishful thinking; there was no escaping his fate.

Today he would go into school, there would be a small presentation and party, and then he would have to say goodbye to his fellow teachers and his beloved pupils for the last time.

Jerome was a widower who lived alone since his wife, Martha, had passed away five years previously. His son, Edward, had immigrated to Australia and was settled there now with a family of his own. Jerome had always been dedicated to teaching, but after his wife's death he had really thrown himself into the job: it was the only thing that kept him going. He had tried his best to persuade the powers that be to let him keep on teaching for another year or two, but they told him that, unfortunately, there was nothing they could do for him: sixty-five was the official retirement age and that was final.

Although Jerome was dreading the day ahead he was determined to keep the best side out so that nobody would guess how he was really feeling. After he had his breakfast he dressed in his smartest outfit, combed his hair into place and when he looked at himself in the mirror he was pleased to see that he looked as well as on any other day. When he was satisfied with his preparations he got into his car and drove the two miles to the school. The morning classes went by in a more or less similar fashion to every other day. The atmosphere in the room, however, was different. Not only was Mr. O'Shaughnessy sad to be leaving, but the pupils, who were for the most part very fond of him, found it hard to believe that this was the last time he would stand in front of the class as their teacher.

At two o'clock the board of directors and the parents arrived and the official retirement ceremony took place. Jerome was thanked for a lifetime of dedicated service and presented with several gifts to mark his retirement. He then went on to make a short speech in which he thanked everyone for their kindness. After that all he had to do was cut the cake and the rest of the afternoon was spent eating, drinking and socialising with officials, parents and pupils. All too soon the party came to an end and it was time to go home. Jerome had somehow managed to keep a smile on his face throughout the afternoon. However, when he returned to his home that evening and closed the door behind him the smile soon disappeared. With no job to go to on Monday morning and no-one to share his retirement with him, he didn't think he would ever smile again.

During the days and weeks which followed Jerome made an effort to adjust to his new life but he found it extremely difficult. For the first few mornings he got up at the usual time but then he began to wonder what the point was; the days were so long with no-one to talk to and nowhere to go. Gradually, he got into the habit of lying on in bed later and later each morning; sometimes he wouldn't stir until midday or even later. He also found that his appetite wasn't what it used to be. He just couldn't be bothered to cook for himself and all too often he ended up with a cup of tea and a sandwich instead of a proper meal. Jerome was aware that all these bad habits were taking a toll on both his physical and mental health, but somehow he just didn't seem to care.

The only thing which kept him going during those difficult months was the fact that his son had promised to come home from Australia for Christmas bringing his wife and two children with him. Edward had immigrated seven years previously and had not been home since. It was now October and Jerome began to think that maybe he should spruce up the house a bit for his visitors. This was good for him; it gave him something to concentrate on instead of thinking about his own misfortunes all the time. For the next month he kept himself busy every day cleaning, tidying and adding a lick of paint anywhere he thought it was needed. He was already beginning to feel better about himself. Perhaps, he thought, there are still some good times ahead.

Then one cold, dreary day in late November disaster struck. Jerome was having his morning cuppa in the kitchen when he heard the postman drop a letter on the mat in the hall. Seeing it was from his son he felt a twinge of excitement. When he sat down at the table and opened it, however, he got an unmerciful shock; Edward was terribly sorry but he wouldn't be able to come home for Christmas, after all. He went on to explain that he had recently lost his job and he now had to dedicate all his time and energy to getting a new one. He said they were all disappointed about not being able to come to Ireland as planned, but with a bit of luck, they'd make the trip either in the summer or the following Christmas.

Jerome was devastated by this news; he felt as if his whole world had collapsed around him. The one event he'd been looking forward to during those long, cold, winter months was now not going to happen. All his preparations had been for nothing; he would now spend Christmas day all alone in his little bungalow with not a sinner to care if he was dead or alive. From that moment on things began to go downhill for him again. He slipped back into his old habits of lying in bed half the day and generally neglecting himself. He knew he should pay a visit to his doctor to get treatment for his depression, but he was just too proud to admit there was anything the matter.

In the second week of January the weather was extremely cold and windy and it rained non-stop for a whole week. Jerome was feeling dreadful as he hadn't been able to go outside his house for several days. On this particular night as he lay in bed listening to the wind and rain on the window he couldn't go to sleep. During the long hours of the night all kinds of disturbing thoughts were going through his head. If only he could go back to the good times when Martha was alive, and he had been a useful member of society teaching the children in the local school. Why, he wondered, had everything he cared about been taken away from him? Even his son, whom he had been so close to in the past, couldn't make the effort to pay him a visit. As the dawn began to break he could lie there no longer, so he got up, put on his clothes and went outside. It was a bitterly cold morning, but the wind and rain had abated.

He started walking, and before he realised it he found himself standing on the little bridge which crossed the river about a mile from his house. As he stared into the murky water of the rain-swollen river for a moment he wondered what he was doing there, but suddenly he knew; this had been at the back of his mind for a long time. All he had to do was take one step off the side of the bridge and it would all be over. He'd have no more long sleepless nights to worry about, and with a bit of luck he'd be reunited with his beloved Martha once again. It seemed the perfect solution to all his troubles. Just as he was thinking there would be nobody around at this time of morning to intervene, he heard a voice behind him.

"Good Morning, Mr. O'Shaughnessy."

He spun round and was astonished to see one of his ex-pupils, Daniel Buckley, who was about ten years old, approaching the bridge with a fishing rod slung over his shoulder and carrying in his hand a small can.

"Good Morning Daniel," he managed to reply, "You're out early, aren't you?" "Yes Sir, I've come to do a bit of fishing."

Without another word, Daniel sauntered onto the bridge and standing beside Jerome attached a worm to the fishing line and cast it into the water. Jerome thought he must be dreaming. Just a few minutes ago a terrible plan had been forming in his head; now he was standing here watching a young boy fishing. Jerome remembered Daniel well from his teaching days. He was one of those pupils who had found learning exceedingly difficult. When he retired these were the children he worried about most. He had always gone out of his way to give them that little bit of extra attention so that they wouldn't fall behind completely. He often wondered if the new teacher would have the same interest in them; he hoped he would, but somehow he didn't think so.

"How are you getting on in school?" he asked Daniel.

"Not very well, Sir. The new teacher doesn't like me and a few others in the class."

"What makes you think he doesn't like you?"

"He never bothers to explain things the way you used to, and then when we're not able to do the homework he says we're stupid. I wish you could come back and be our teacher again; school would be so much better."

When Jerome said goodbye to Daniel and walked back to his house that morning a new plan was already forming in his mind. Wouldn't it be great, he thought, if I could run a sort of homework club in the school each afternoon where those pupils who require extra tuition and help could avail of it. A few days later he proposed his plan to the school principal who thought it was an excellent idea. He'd have to call a meeting of the board of directors, of course, and get their approval. Fortunately, the board of directors agreed, and Jerome got the go-ahead for his homework club.

Years later, when Daniel Buckley had completed his college education, Jerome was invited to his graduation. Mrs Buckley thanked him for all he had done for her son and other young people in the village:

"Only for all the help you gave him over the years, Daniel wouldn't be getting his degree today." she said. "I don't know how he can ever repay you for your kindness."
"Daniel owes me nothing," replied Mr.

O'Shaughnessy, "Let's not go into the details, as it all happened a long time ago, but only for your son, there's a strong possibility I wouldn't be here to see this day. Can we just leave it at that?"

"Ok," replied Mrs Buckley, "if that's the way you want it. But there's one thing I must insist on."

"What's that?"

"Whether you like it or not, you're going to join us in the hotel for a slap up meal to celebrate the occasion."

"That's something I have no objection to whatsoever." he smiled. "Let's go!"

SUSPICIONS

Seventy-five year old Bob Johnson lived alone in a dilapidated old farmhouse that had seen better days. It was situated on a hundred-acre farm which had been in the Johnson family for many generations, handed down from father to son. Born in the nineteen-forties, Bob had seen many changes over the years. Although now he suffered from the usual aches and pains which accompany old age, his memory was as sharp as ever.

Some of his earliest memories were of attending the local school with his two older sisters. Later, when they married and moved out, he remained at home with his parents working on the farm. In those days, the Johnsons were among the best off farmers in the county. His father, William, was always referred to as Mr. Johnson by the labouring classes who depended on him and his likes for a day's work so that they could feed and clothe their children.

Then in the sixties disaster struck. Mr. Johnson, who had never been sick a day in his life, suffered a massive heart attack and died. Now there was nobody left to run the farm only Bob and his mother. Although Bob had always been his father's right-hand man, he never took much interest in the business side of things. He was only twenty and he had thought there was plenty of time before he'd have to worry about anything like that. His mother wasn't much use either, as she had always devoted her time to running the house and looking after the children.

The farm had never been as prosperous again after that, but they carried on as best they could. Then in the nineteen-eighties, Mrs. Johnston's health began to deteriorate, and a few years later she, too, passed away. Bob was left all alone in the big, old, rambling farmhouse. Now in his early forties, he considered himself too old to get married, so he settled into a solitary existence and soon became known as a confirmed bachelor. For the next thirty-five years he lived alone with only the cats and dogs to keep him company in the long winter nights.

Although he was now getting on in years, Bob was extremely independent. However, he was aware he wasn't going to live forever, and sooner or later he'd have to hand over to the next generation. He had several relatives who'd be only too glad to take over the farm, but he had already decided to leave it to one of his grand-nephews called Eamonn. From the time he was a young lad Eamonn had always showed an interest in farming, and he was always there to help out when needed, so he knew he'd be leaving it in good hands.

One summer when Eamonn had some time to spare he offered to tidy up the old farmyard for Bob as it had become very run-down over the years. First, he cleaned out all the rubbish which had accumulated in the outhouses and sheds, and then he applied a good coat of paint to everything. Down at the far end of the yard, out of sight of the house, was a large pile of stones which didn't seem to be serving any useful purpose. Eamonn suggested moving them and perhaps they could build another shed there sometime in the future. However, Bob didn't seem too keen on the idea. Underneath the stones, he explained, was an old well which had supplied water to the house in years gone by. When he was about ten years old he came home from school one evening to find that the well had been covered over with a pile of stones. There had been no explanation, but his father had warned him never to go near it again as it would bring him bad luck.

That night when Eamonn had gone home Bob sat all alone by the big open fireplace in the kitchen thinking about what he should do. Should he let his grand-nephew go ahead and clear away the pile of stones, or should he continue to heed his father's warning and stay away from it altogether? He had a lot to think about. As he stared into the flames he couldn't help wondering, not for the first time, if there was a connection between the covering up of the well and another incident which happened around the same time.

In an old, dilapidated house just down the road from Johnsons lived Jack and Ellie Murphy and their large family. Jack could only get an odd day's work here and there, and there was never enough money to feed and clothe them all. The children would often come up to the farmhouse in the hope of getting something to eat. One day one of the little girls, Sarah, who was about six at the time came in. Bob's mother didn't mind giving her a slice of bread and jam, but she wasn't the sort of woman to give something for nothing, so she sent her down to the well for a bucket of water. After about twenty minutes there was no sign of her coming back, so she went down herself. Sometime later, she came back alone with the water saying that Sarah had gone home.

Shortly afterwards Bob heard that Sarah had been sent to live with her uncle and aunt in England; they had no family themselves and had decided to ease the burden by taking one of the children and rearing her as their own. Bob never heard Sarah's name mentioned again. Could it have been possible that Sarah had fallen into the well that day and drowned? Perhaps his mother was afraid that she'd be blamed for what happened. After all, who in their right mind would send a six year old child to draw water from a deep well on her own? But if that were the case, why would her family have said she'd gone to live in England? That made no sense at all.

Then he remembered something else which he had never really thought much about before. About six months after the incidents with Sarah and the covering in of the well, a new house was built on Mr. Johnston's land. As soon as it was completed the Murphy family left their old, ramshackle house and moved into the new one. And that wasn't all; Mr. Johnston took Jack Murphy on as a full-time employee where he remained for the rest of his working days. He had no proof, of course, but the more Bob thought about it, the more certain he was that a terrible tragedy had taken place and been covered up by both families.

Bob sat late into the night thinking about what he should do until he eventually made up his mind. The next day he told Eamonn he had decided to continue to abide by his father's wishes and leave the well undisturbed. "After I'm gone," he said, "you can do whatever you like with it." The subject was never mentioned again during Bob's lifetime, and when he passed away a few years later he took his suspicions with him to the grave.

A SECOND CHANCE

Everyone wondered what had come over Dinny Lacey. As he cycled around the parish that morning delivering the post, he greeted all and sundry with a smile and a friendly word. For thirty years Dinny had been a familiar figure on the highways and byways delivering letters, and the occasional parcel, to the people of Dunmore. While he had always been respected for his honesty and integrity, he was usually quiet and reserved in his manner, and no one had ever seen him smile or engage in idle chat. There was, however, a simple explanation for Dinny's sudden change of mood. While listening to the death notices on the local radio that morning he had learned that a wealthy farmer, Thomas Smith, who lived in the next parish, had passed away suddenly. It wasn't that he was a relative who might leave him something in his will, or anything like that. No, Dinny had a different reason entirely for rejoicing over the sudden demise of Mr. Smith.

Dinny was the youngest of three boys. He was born and reared in the small cottage where he still lived on the outskirts of the village. His father died when he was twelve, and a few years later his two older brothers immigrated to America where they made a good life for themselves. When he was eighteen Dinny would have loved to have followed his siblings across the Atlantic, but everyone said it was his duty to stay and look after his mother, so that's what he did. When he left school he found employment in a hardware store in the village. Then a couple of years later he applied for and got a job as the local postman. His mother was thrilled that a son of hers had secured a permanent and pensionable position with the Department of

Posts and Telegraphs. No one belonging to her had ever had such a position before, and she never tired of bragging about him to anyone who was willing to listen.

He soon settled into his new job. What he liked most about it was that, from the time he collected the letters from the post office in the morning until he arrived back in the evening, he was his own boss with nobody to order him around or tell him what to do. He was young and fit, and it was a pleasure to be out in the fresh air all day cycling around the countryside on the new bicycle provided for him by the Department. What more could he ask for? Of course the weather wasn't always ideal, but once he was kitted out with the proper rain gear he didn't mind too much. Every job had some drawbacks, he thought, and a shower of rain here and there was a small price to pay for all the benefits he enjoyed.

Another advantage of the job was that he had plenty of free time. In the evenings after work and at the weekends Dinny played hurling and football with the local club. And, of course, like all the other young people in the area, he liked to go dancing. It was now the nineteen-fifties and dancehalls were becoming a popular places for young people to socialize. It was at one of these dances that he met Peggy O'Neill. The moment he first laid eyes on Peggy, with her dark hair and blue eyes, he thought she was the most beautiful girl he had ever seen. Somehow he plucked up the courage to ask her to dance, and before the music stopped he knew he was in love with her. Luckily, the feeling was mutual, and it wasn't long until the pair of them were going out together on a regular basis.

For the next year or so Dinny was the happiest he'd ever been in his life. He was working in a job he loved, and he was going out with the best-looking girl in the parish. Although he was sure that Peggy and himself would one day get married, they hadn't got round to talking seriously about their future yet. Dinny didn't want to propose to her until he could afford to present her with an expensive engagement ring. With this purpose in mind he began to save a few pounds from his wages each week. However, as he was only a short time in the job, he wasn't earning a lot, so he knew it'd be a while before he could buy the ring he felt she deserved. In the meantime, however, they continued to enjoy spending time together.

One night when they had been going out for about a year they went to a dance in the village hall. As they stood chatting to some of their friends between dances, a tall, good-looking man whom they had never seen before came over and asked Peggy to dance. Not wishing to be rude, and seeing no reason why she should refuse, she accepted the invitation. A few seconds later the band started playing and Peggy and the stranger were soon gliding around the floor in time to the music. Dinny continued to talk to his friends while at the same time keeping one eye on the dancers. Every time Peggy and her partner passed by, he noticed they were laughing and chatting just like old friends. After what seemed like an eternity the music stopped, and Peggy came back. Dinny was annoyed, but he tried not to show it. Later that night, however, he caught Peggy and her dance partner smiling at each other across the hall a couple of times. He pretended not to notice as he didn't want to appear jealous, but he had a feeling that his life was about to take a turn for the worse; and he was right.

Dinny and Peggy continued to see each other for a while after that, but somehow things didn't feel the same between them. Then one day, a friend of Dinny's had some upsetting news; Peggy was cheating on him. She'd been spotted in a pub a few miles from home with Thomas Smith who was a wealthy farmer's son from the next parish. The next time they met Dinny asked her about it, and she admitted it was true; Thomas Smith was the man who had asked her to dance in the village hall a few weeks previously. Peggy told Dinny she was terribly sorry; she never meant to hurt him, but their relationship was over.

Dinny was devastated; he couldn't believe that the girl he hoped to marry had abandoned him for someone else. His friends tried to console him saying he was better off without her, and there was plenty more fish in the sea. No matter what they said, however, it was no use. He blamed himself for the break-up, and he tormented himself day and night trying to figure out what he had done wrong. Three months later he heard that, not only had Peggy and Thomas got engaged, but he had bought her one of the most expensive engagement rings ever seen in that part of the country. Shortly after that they were married, and she left the village to set up home with her new husband.

After Peggy had disappeared from his life Dinny became almost a different person. His heart was broken, and he swore he'd never go out with another woman as long as he lived. He gave up the hurling and football, and for the next twenty years he dedicated all his energy to his work and looking after his mother until she passed away.

Now, here he was cycling around the parish greeting everyone with a big smile on his face. And why wouldn't he? Thomas Smith, the man you had taken the love of his life away from him all those years ago, was gone to his eternal reward, which meant that

Peggy was a free woman again. They were both still young, in their early forties, so he decided he'd have another go at winning her heart. This time, however, he'd have to be more careful; he didn't want to make the same mistake as before and let somebody else run off with her again.

Over the following days he tried to come up with a plan. The first thing he'd have to do was buy the engagement ring. Then he could go to see her and make his proposal. Suddenly, it dawned on him that he'd have to start saving for the ring again, as he had very little put aside. At first, he thought he might be able to get a loan from somebody, but he didn't really want to do that as he was reluctant to let anyone know his business. If only there was some way he could get his hands on a few pounds as quickly as possible.

Suddenly an idea struck him. In those days, several people from the village and surrounding areas went to work in England and sent home money to their parents or wives and families at the end of each month. They'd usually enclose a postal order or cheque but there were also a few who still sent cash. Dinny always knew by the feel of the letter if there was cash enclosed. What if he opened the odd letter here and there and took out the money; would he be discovered or would he get away with it? It had never occurred to him to do anything like this before; he'd always been as honest as the sun. Now that he had the idea in his head, however, he couldn't get rid of it, and in the end he gave in to the temptation. The first time he did it was the worst; he couldn't believe he was actually stealing money. But after that it got easier. When he'd find a letter containing cash he'd slip it into the inside pocket of his jacket. Then, when he got home, he'd take out the money and burn the letter.

A couple of months passed by, and Dinny had a nice sum of money piled up under the mattress. Surely, he thought, I have enough now to buy the ring. It was only then it dawned on him that the money was in sterling – he'd have to take it to the bank to exchange it for Irish pounds. The bank manager, being a suspicious sort, wondered where Dinny had gotten all this English money from, so he decided to have a discreet word with the garda sergeant. As soon as the sergeant heard this he was in no doubt about what was happening. He'd had several complaints from people recently about letters from England going missing. The sergeant found it difficult to believe that Dinny would do anything of that sort; he'd been so honest all his life. However, when the guards came to his house and questioned him he got such a shock that he admitted everything. Shortly afterwards there was a court case where he was ordered to give back all the money he'd stolen, and he was sentenced to six months in prison.

The following months were a nightmare for Dinny. He couldn't come to terms with life in prison, and he couldn't understand how he could have been so stupid to do what he had done and think he could get away with it. As bad as his life was before, he had now made everything ten times worse. When he'd be released from prison he'd have no job, and he'd be known as a jailbird for the rest of his life. There was no light at the end of the tunnel as far as he could see, and sometimes he even wished he could end it all.

Then, one day when he was feeling particularly low he got a pleasant surprise. Peggy arrived at the prison to visit him. She told him she'd always loved him, and she knew a month after her marriage to Thomas Smith that she'd made the biggest mistake of her life. To his amazement she asked him if he would marry her now. He said of course he would, but he still had no money to buy her an engagement ring; did that not bother her?

"Not a bit," she replied. "I don't want any engagement ring; I had one of those before and it didn't bring me happiness. All I want this time is the man I should have married twenty years ago."

When Peggy left, Dinny went back to his cell with a big smile on his face. There was a month of his prison term left, but that didn't bother him. Now that he knew Peggy and himself were going to get married at last, he felt sure that, despite all the ups and downs in his life so far, the best was yet to come.

THE MISSING BRACELET

Sixteen year old Sally O'Leary was both nervous and excited as she walked the half mile from her home to Rochford Manor where she was due to start work that morning. Sally was the eldest of a large family who lived on the estate belonging to Lord and Lady Rochford. Her father, Johnny, leased a few acres from the landlord where he produced barely enough to feed himself and his family. She was nervous because she had no idea how the gentry lived or what she would be expected to do. On the other hand, she had just finished school and felt very lucky to have been offered this job. There were plenty of other girls in the locality who'd give their right arm for such an opportunity.

The first week or two in her new position were the most difficult; there was so much to be learned. However, she was lucky that the housekeeper, Mrs. Smith, was a patient soul who explained everything and helped her to settle into her new surroundings. At the end of the first month Lady Rochford informed her that her work was satisfactory, and she could now consider herself part of the staff. Sally was over the moon. Although she was only the maid-of-all-work and on the bottom rung of the ladder, she had the chance to work her way up and eventually make something of herself. And that wasn't the only benefit; she was now in a position to contribute to the family's income, which was badly needed.

The weeks and months passed quickly by and Sally was now familiar with all the routines which made up the running of the household. No matter what happened the rest of the week, Monday was always washday. Each of the staff had a part to play in this ritual, including Mrs. Smith, herself. Among other tasks, Sally had to take the freshly washed clothes and hang them on the line which was situated in a small paddock some distance from the house. One day as she pegged the clothes in position, she suddenly saw Frederick, son of the Lord and Lady of the Manor, ride his horse through the gate at the far side of the paddock and straight over to where she stood. And that was how it all started.

What began as a casual encounter between two young people at the clothesline slowly turned into something more serious. While Frederick, who was seventeen, was aware that associating with the maid-of-all-work in his mother's household would be frowned upon, it didn't stop him from falling for Sally. As their relationship progressed, they somehow managed to keep it secret; there was only one other person who knew what was going on and that was Frederick's little sister, Ruth, who was only seven years old at the time.

They had now been seeing each other for six months and it was coming up to Sally's seventeenth birthday. Frederick wanted to give her something special to celebrate the occasion but he had no money. Although his parents were wealthy they were both tight-fisted and seldom gave their children pocket-money. Then, out of the blue, an opportunity presented itself. One evening Frederick went into the downstairs bathroom to wash his face and hands before dinner. As he combed his hair, his eyes fell on a bright object which was lying on a shelf above the handbasin. Out of curiosity he picked it up and saw that it was a magnificent gold bracelet.

At that moment, several thoughts raced through Frederick's mind. He guessed, not only by the weight, but also by the old-world look and feel of the bracelet, that it was valuable. He was fairly certain that it belonged to his mother; she must have taken it off to wash her hands and forgotten to put it back on. But the uppermost thought in his mind at that moment was not how much it was worth, or even who it belonged to, but how elegant it would look on Sally's dainty wrist. Without any thought as to the possible consequences of his actions, he slipped the bracelet into his pocket and joined the rest of the family for dinner.

A few days later when Frederick presented Sally with the bracelet on her birthday she was stunned.

"It's gorgeous," she declared, as he placed it on her wrist. "I didn't think I'd ever be the owner of anything so delightful. It must have cost you a fortune".

"Well actually, I, I... didn't buy it."

Sally was aghast, "Where did you get it?"

"I found it; I think it belongs to my mother."

"Oh Frederick, you shouldn't have taken it. You'll have to give it back."

"Don't be silly, it's been a few days now and she hasn't missed it. Anyway she has so much jewelry she'll never get around to wearing it all."

The last thing Sally wanted to do was to hurt Frederick's feelings so, against her better judgement, she gave in and agreed to keep the bracelet.

"I don't think it'd be a good idea to wear it right now," she said, "but I'll keep it in my room and every time I look at it I'll think of you."

But, unfortunately, that wasn't the end of the matter. A month later Lady Rochford decided to carry out a stock take of all her possessions. She had everything of value in the house recorded in a catalogue along with a corresponding photograph. It was only when she realised that the bracelet was missing that she remembered leaving it in the bathroom. All members of the household staff were questioned but, of course, nobody owned up. While Lady Rochford had no hesitation in suspecting the servants of stealing, it never even crossed her mind that one of her own family could be guilty. However, somebody had to take the blame, and because it was Sally's job to clean the bathroom first thing every morning, Lady Rochford decided she was the culprit. She said she had no choice but to dismiss her; she couldn't possibly keep a dishonest employee under her roof. Sally was devastated, but there was nothing she could do; this was in the early nineteen hundreds and there was no such thing as "unfair dismissal" in those days.

A few days later when Frederick found out that Sally had been dismissed for stealing the bracelet he was distraught, knowing that it was all his fault. Although he did try to get his mother to change her mind pointing out that she had no proof that Sally was the culprit, he didn't have the courage to own up to the theft himself. A dreadful argument arose between Frederick and his mother, which ended with him storming out of the house. That was the last time she saw him alive. Spurred on by a mixture of anger and guilt, he rushed to the stable, mounted his horse and set off at a mad gallop across the hills. Unfortunately, it ended in disaster; travelling at breakneck speed the horse tripped and fell, and both of them were killed instantly. And thus ended the brief romantic interlude which had taken place between Fredrick Rochford and Sally O'Leary.

From that day onwards Sally had no further dealings with the inhabitants of the manor house. She was heartbroken by Frederick's death, but she tried as best she could to put the past behind her and move on with her life. Although she never told anyone about her relationship with Frederick, she kept the bracelet as it was the only thing she had to remind her of their love for each other. She never wore it but decided that if she ever had a daughter of her own she'd give it to her, perhaps on her twenty-first birthday or another special occasion.

That wasn't to be, however. Sally did eventually meet and marry a young man from her own social class and they had two sons but no daughters. In due time, however, she became the proud grandmother of two grandsons and, her pride and joy, her granddaughter, Emma. Sally doted on her granddaughter, and Emma was equally attached to her. In nineteen seventy, just a month before Emma's twenty-first birthday, Sally became very ill. Before she passed away she gave the bracelet to Emma and made her promise to wear it to the party which her parents were planning for her.

"I won't be there in person, but I want you to promise me to wear the bracelet so that you'll feel I am with you in spirit.

"Of course I will, gran," promised Emma, as she tried to hold back the tears.

Emma adored her new bracelet and from that time on she rarely left the house without it. One night she was at a dance in the hotel in the town with her boyfriend. As they relaxed at the bar with a drink some of her friends came over and admired the exquisite bracelet. Emma was thrilled and told them how her beloved grandmother had given it to her before she died. Suddenly, a well-dressed gentleman who was sitting nearby approached her and asked if he could have a look. Emma held out her hand to give him a close-up view of the bracelet. He stared at it for what seemed like a very long time.

"It's a magnificent bracelet," he said, "but I'm sorry to have to tell you it doesn't belong to you."

Emma looked at him in dismay. "What do you mean, it doesn't belong to me? Of course it does. It was given to me by my late grandmother before she died. Are you trying to say she stole it, or something?"

"I'm not saying she stole it. All I know is that bracelet belonged to my grandmother, who was Lady Rochford. There's a picture of it in the family catalogue with a note which states it disappeared from the house in the year nineteen hundred and ten and has never been recovered."

Emma declared she had never heard anything so ridiculous in all her life. However, the man, who said his name was Henry Rochford, heir to the manor house, assured her it was no joke and she would be hearing further from him. A few minutes later he finished his drink and left. When he was gone Emma and her boyfriend had a good laugh about the whole thing; surely he'd made a mistake, and they'd hear no more about it.

It didn't end there, however. A couple of weeks later Emma received a letter from Henry Rochford's solicitor restating what he had said and advising her to return the bracelet immediately if she didn't want to be dragged through the courts. The last thing she wanted was to have to appear before a judge and jury, so she reluctantly decided to send it back. Emma was heartbroken to have to part with the beautiful gift her grandmother had given her, but there was nothing she could do about it; she was sure she'd never see it again.

A week later a rather posh car drove up to Emma's house and an elderly couple got out and knocked on the door. When her mother opened it they introduced themselves as Ruth and Theodore from Rochford Manor and asked if they could see Emma. She brought them into the living room and invited them to sit down. Emma wondered what they wanted. The lady was the first to speak.

"You don't know me Emma," she said, "my name is Ruth Rochford and I'm the present owner of Rochford Manor. This is my husband, Theodore."

"It's nice to meet you both," replied Emma.

"I'd like to give you this," she said, handing Emma a small black box.

"What is it?"

"Why don't you open it and see?"

Emma opened the box and there on a velvet cushion was the bracelet she thought she'd never see again.

"It's the bracelet! But I don't understand. Why are you giving it to me?" Doesn't it belong to Rochford Manor?"

Ruth explained that she was a seven year old child when Sally O'Leary came to work at Rochford Manor. She soon became very close to Sally as she often took care of her when her mother, Lady Rochford, was out socialising with her numerous friends. Then one day she came across her brother, Frederick, to whom she was also very close, kissing Sally, and they made her promise not to tell anyone about their relationship. Ruth was thrilled to be part of such an exciting secret and she hoped that someday they'd get married so that Sally and she could be "real sisters".

Everything was great for a while, but then suddenly it all went wrong. It started when the bracelet went missing. Then Sally was dismissed. And, as if that wasn't bad enough, her beloved brother, Frederick, was killed off his horse. Her whole life was turned upside down. In fact she said, reaching for his hand, she never knew happiness again until she met her dear husband, Theodore. Ruth went on to say she didn't believe that it was Sally who had stolen the bracelet; it was more likely that Frederick took it and gave it to her. "Of course, we'll never know for sure now," she sighed.

"Whichever way it happened, the bracelet is yours now to do what you like with. You can sell it or keep it – the choice is yours."

A year later when Emma got married she invited Ruth and Theodore to the wedding. As Emma walked down the aisle with her new husband, Ruth was pleased to see her wearing the bracelet which sparkled in the sunshine streaming through the window of the church. She hoped Sally and Frederick were looking down, and that they too were happy to know that the bracelet had found a deserving home at last.

SARAH'S LEGACY

Sarah Maloney was an only child who was born in the year eighteen ninety in a rural townland in the south-east of Ireland. Times were hard and money was scarce, but nonetheless, she had a happy childhood growing up in the countryside and attending the local national school. When Sarah was fourteen, the old schoolmaster retired and a new teacher named Maurice O'Shea from Galway was to take his place. Mr. O'Shea, a young man in his twenties, moved into the teacher's accommodation attached to the school and took up his new appointment in September.

The new teacher settled in well and the children soon became accustomed to his ways. They all agreed that he was friendly and good-humoured and, more importantly, he wasn't too fond of the cane; there was, however, more to Mr. O'Shea than met the eye. In those days it wasn't unusual for children to stay in school until they were fifteen, as that was the only education available to them. At fourteen, not only was Sarah the oldest girl in the school, but she was also by far the most attractive. Tall and slim, with long, dark hair and blue eyes, she looked way older than her years, and it wasn't long until she caught the roving eye of Maurice O'Shea.

Sarah, being the innocent country girl that she was, enjoyed all the attention he lavished on her. When he began asking her to stay back after school to help him tidy up and prepare for the following day, neither she nor her parents thought anything of it. In fact, they were pleased; surely it was no harm, they thought, to be "in" with the teacher. Perhaps he might be able to help her get a job when she left school. However, Mr. O'Shea had other things on his mind, and before long, instead of cleaning and tidying the schoolroom, as she was supposed to be doing, Sarah was sharing his bed. She was over the moon; she had never had a boyfriend before, and now here she was in a real relationship with this gorgeous, mature man in his twenties.

There was, however, one thing which she thought was strange; he warned her not to tell anyone.

"Why not?" she asked, disappointed.
"Because I'm the teacher and you're my pupil. It wouldn't be appropriate for us to have a relationship."
"So, it'll be ok next year when I leave school, we can tell everyone then?"
"Yes, yes, of course," he replied without looking at her, and that was the end of the conversation.

Unfortunately for Sarah, there was to be no happy ending to this fairy-tale. Three months later when she started to feel unwell, her mother took her to the doctor who confirmed she was pregnant. Her parents were outraged and marched her down to Mr. O'Shea's house to confront him. At first he tried to deny all responsibility, but when they threatened to go to the police he changed his tune.

"Alright, what do you want me to do?"
"Well," said her father, "there are two things we want from you. First, you'll give Sarah a payment of a hundred pounds, and second, you'll leave this place and never show your face around here again.
"And what if I don't agree?"
"If you don't agree, I'll go straight to the police and tell them everything. You'll probably end up in jail and you'll never teach again; it'll be the end of your career."

When he realised Sarah's father meant business Mr. O'Shea agreed to the conditions. He promised to hand over the money within a few days and to give in his notice immediately. Poor Sarah was distraught. When she tried to have her say, her father warned her to be quiet, and her beloved boyfriend couldn't even look her in the eye. She couldn't believe how things were turning out.

That was the last time Sarah ever laid eyes on Maurice O'Shea. Within a month he'd disappeared from the district and was never heard of again. Sarah's parents kept her hidden away in the house for the rest of her pregnancy, while informing the neighbours she'd gone to work in Dublin. The most important thing, as far as they were concerned, was to keep everything secret; if the truth got out they'd all be ruined. To be fair to her father he didn't keep the hundred pounds for himself, as he could have done, but lodged it in the bank in his daughter's name. At least she'll have something to fall back on, he thought, if times ever get really tough.

The weeks and months dragged slowly by until the following June, when Sarah gave birth to a baby boy. The moment she laid eyes on him she forgot all about the pain and suffering she'd endured, and she felt sure that from now on things were about to get better. She had decided to christen him Fionn after the brave warrior Fionn Mac Cumhaill whom she had learned about in school. That wasn't to be, however; a week after he was born she awoke one morning to find herself staring at an empty cot. She told herself not to panic; he was probably crying and her mother took him so as not to wake her. However, when she went into the kitchen her parents were having their breakfast as usual, but there was no sign of the baby. At that moment a cold hand gripped her heart; she knew something was terribly wrong.

"Where's my baby?"

For a few moments there was silence, then her father spoke. "Sit down Sarah, we need to talk to you."

Sarah somehow found a chair and collapsed into it.

"Where's my baby? What have you done with him?"

"He's gone," said her mother.

"What do you mean, gone?"

"His adoptive parents arrived early this morning to take him to his new home. I know it's hard for you Sarah, but it's the best for everyone. He'll be well looked after and you can get on with your life. And, most importantly, nobody need ever know what happened."

*****

Seventy years later Sarah Maloney still lived in the house where she had grown up. She never got over that terrible time in her life, and after her parents passed away she lived a completely isolated existence. Her only companions were her cat and dog and a small flock of hens which she kept in the fowl house at the bottom of the yard. Most people just left her to her own devices, however there were some who said cruel things about her even going so far as to claim she was a witch. Over the years these malicious rumors had spread and parents warned their children to stay well away from her in case she might cast a spell on them.

Although the children who passed her house on their way to and from school were scared of Sarah, sometimes when a gang of them got together, they'd throw stones at her roof, calling "Witch!, Witch!,". Then they'd run like the wind down the road laughing and never giving a thought to the poor old woman or how she might feel.

There was, however, one little boy who was different from the rest. His name was Tommy and he came somewhere in the middle of a poor family of nine children. Even if he had wanted to be part of the gang who tormented Old Sarah it wouldn't have been possible as he was unable to run away from danger like the others. Born with a disability, one of his legs was shorter than the other which meant that he walked with a pronounced limp. The doctors advised his parents that he could have surgery to fix the problem. Unfortunately, they also informed them that an operation would be quite expensive which meant, of course, it was out of the question.

Tommy knew what it was like to be an outsider. While some of his schoolmates treated him well enough, there were others who teased and bullied him because of his disability. Although he'd heard the stories about Old Sarah being a witch, he didn't believe them. All he could think of was how lonely she must be living all alone with nobody to talk to all day. So, one evening as he walked home from school alone, the others having run on ahead as usual, he plucked up courage and knocked on her door.

At first Sarah was suspicious when she saw the young boy standing on her door-step with a smile on his face. However, when he explained that he had just dropped in to see how she was keeping and if she needed company, she invited him in and even gave him a slice or two of bread and jam. It soon became a habit for Tommy to call in to Sarah for a chat or to do some little job for her on his way home from school. And Sarah began to enjoy the company; in fact, it gave her a whole new lease of life. Instead of sitting alone brooding over the past she now had something to look forward to.

Sarah couldn't help feeling sorry for Tommy who, because of his disability, was unable to run and play like other children. She was now in her mid-eighties and, realising that she couldn't have very long left in this world, she wished there was something she could do for him before she passed away. If she was a rich woman she'd willingly pay for the operation he needed.

One morning while Sarah was out feeding the chickens she saw the postman coming up the road on his bicycle. He won't have anything for me, she thought; her electricity bill had arrived a few days previously and that was almost the only mail she ever received nowadays. She couldn't believe her eyes, therefore, when she saw him coming across the yard towards her with a letter in his hand. As soon as he was gone she took it into the kitchen and tore it open. To her surprise it was from the local bank. Not being very good at reading and also because of her failing eyesight, it took Sarah a while to make sense of the letter. However, after going over it a few times she figured out what it meant.

The hundred pounds which Sarah's father had lodged in her name seventy years ago, which she'd completely forgotten about, was still sitting in the bank awaiting her instructions. The good news was that with all the interest that had been added on over the years there was now over a thousand pounds in her account. It was now the nineteen-seventies and a thousand pounds was a lot of money in those days. The letter went on to explain that she'd have to produce the original bank book which her father would have received when he made the deposit; without that nothing could be done. Oh no, she thought, where am I going to find that? However, with Tommy's help she practically turned the house upside down until eventually she found it in the bottom of an old chest of drawers which hadn't been used for years, and she sent it off to the bank immediately.

There was no doubt in Sarah's mind as to how she was going to spend this windfall that had suddenly come her way: without further ado, Tommy would have his operation. It was a great solace to her to know that the money, which should have been spent on her own child, would make a life changing-difference to another little boy seventy years later.

A BUNCH OF DANDELIONS

On a beautiful sunny morning in mid-April, twenty twenty-one, Nellie sat in her chair outside the nursing home where she had been a resident for several years. She was glad the winter was over and summer was on its way again. Although she was ninety-one years old Nellie enjoyed nothing better than being out here in the fresh air where she could admire the lovely lawns and gardens which surrounded the building. This spring, however, was even more special than all the others. Not only had Nellie survived another winter but she had also lived through a pandemic. For over a year now the residents of the home had been unable to receive their usual visitors. All they could do during that time was wave at each other through a window which wasn't the same at all. However, that was all over now. Two weeks ago Nellie had received the long awaited vaccine, and today she was to have her first face-to-face visit from her granddaughter and great-grandson.

At eleven o'clock Nellie was delighted to see her granddaughter, Emily, hurrying up the avenue with her four year old son, Jack, by the hand. They greeted each other warmly and Emily sat down to have a chat with her beloved grandmother. For a few minutes Jack sat quietly by his mother's side, but it wasn't long until he got bored listening to the chit-chat of the two women, so he got up and wandered around in search of something more interesting to amuse himself with. The two women were so engrossed in their conversation they took little notice of him; as long as he was quiet, that was all that mattered.

About fifteen minutes later Jack suddenly

came back to where they were sitting. In his hand he carried a small bunch of golden yellow dandelions. Going up to his great-grandmother he placed them on her lap and said:

"Nana, I picked these for you, I hope you like them."

Nellie was taken aback; it was so long since anyone had given her flowers.

"Thank you Jack, they're my favourite flowers in the whole world," she declared as the tears ran down her face.

Emily felt terrible when she saw her grandmother crying. She wished now that she had remembered to buy her some proper flowers on the way here. No wonder she's upset, she thought; she's spent a whole year in isolation, and all she gets at the end of it is a bunch of weeds! Moving closer to her Nana she put her arm around her and tried to comfort her.

"Don't be upset, Nana," she pleaded, "I promise to bring you some proper flowers the next time I come."

Nellie smiled through her tears. "Oh no, I'm

not upset," she said, "I meant it when I said these are my favourite flowers."

Emily didn't understand. "But how can that be, sure they're nothing but a bunch of weeds."

"They might be weeds to some people, but if you have a few minutes to spare I'll tell you why they mean so much to me."

Nellie was born in the year nineteen thirty. She was the eldest in a family of four and grew up on a tiny farm in the west of Ireland. Times were hard and money was scarce, so when her father got the chance to join the British army in nineteen forty he took it and went off to fight in France. When he was gone Nellie's mother had to run the farm and rear the children which was no easy task for a woman on her own. Nellie and her younger siblings soon got used to helping out around the farm and when they came home from school in the evenings there was always an endless list of jobs waiting to be done.

Then one day in the autumn of nineteen forty-four, when Nellie was fourteen, her mother received a telegram in which she was regretfully informed that her husband was missing in action, presumed dead. That was all they could tell her. They assured her that they would be in contact with her again when further information became available. Nellie's mother was inconsolable. This was the worst news she could possibly receive, just when she'd thought the worst was over and her husband would be coming home to her soon. While Nellie was also devastated, it didn't seem to affect the younger members of the family as much. After all, they hadn't seen their father for four years; it wasn't the same as if he'd been around every day.

The weeks and months which followed were difficult for everyone. However, with the help of good neighbours and extended family, they somehow managed to get through the dark months of winter. Every day Nellie's mother was expecting to hear more information about what had happened to her husband, but no more telegrams arrived. Then in the spring of nineteen forty-five something wonderful happened. They had arrived home from school and were all seated around the table in the kitchen having their dinner when there was a knock at the door. This was strange as nobody ever called at that time of day. When Nellie's mother opened the door who was standing there but her husband, the man she thought she'd never see again. At first she wondered if he was a ghost, but when he smiled at her she knew he was real. Whoever that telegram was meant for, she thought, it certainly wasn't for me.

"So, you decided to come home at last," she said pretending to be mad at him.
"I just thought I'd come and see how you are all doing, and I even brought you a bouquet of flowers." Grinning mischievously, he held out a small bunch of dandelions which he had picked from the roadside on his way up to the house.
"Ah, never mind your dandelions," she said as she threw her arms around him, "come here and give us a kiss."

Nellie had never felt so happy in all her life. Later, as her father sat at the table chatting to her mother and getting to know his family again, Nellie took the bunch of dandelions and instead of throwing them out, put them into an old jug with some water, and placed them in the kitchen window. To her, at that moment, they were the most beautiful flowers in the world. Every spring after that when the golden, yellow dandelions appeared in the hedgerows and fields they reminded her of the day her father had come back into their lives like a ray of sunshine.

When Nellie finished her story she looked down at the bunch of dandelions which Jack had picked for her.

"So now you see why this little bouquet means so much to me," she smiled, "in fact, I couldn't have asked for a better present."

BIDDY O'FLAHERTY'S SHOP

O'Flaherty's shop was situated on the outskirts of the town of Doonmore. Built by Edward O'Flaherty in the early nineteen hundreds, it had seen many changes down through the years. In the early days of its existence, when the town had been a mere village with a handful of houses, it was the main grocery and hardware store in the area, supplying not only the needs of the villagers, but also the farmers and cottagers of the surrounding countryside. When Edward died in nineteen thirty the shop was taken over by his son, Thomas, who carried on the business until his death in nineteen sixty-three. Since then it had been run by Thomas's daughter, Biddy.

It was now the year two thousand and sixteen, and Biddy was a sprightly eighty-one year old. Having worked in the shop from the time she was big enough to peek over the counter, she had no intention of retiring anytime soon. She had, however, cut back on the variety of goods she sold and now concentrated mainly on groceries and sweets. While still selling a fair quantity of groceries, her main customers were the children who passed by her shop on the way to and from school each day. She enjoyed their company immensely, and she hoped she'd be serving them for a long time to come.

Despite Biddy's shop remaining more or less unchanged for over a hundred years, the same couldn't be said for the town of Doonmore. The population had increased dramatically and there were several new housing estates where cattle and sheep had once grazed peacefully. Along with the increase in population had come supermarkets, clothes shops and hardware stores. The main street of the town being narrow, the place soon became congested with cars, vans and lorries. This was bad for business, profits deteriorated and the powers that be decided that something would have to be done about it.

After several meetings of the town council, the chairman, Mr. Higginbottom, and his colleagues decided to build a ring road around the town which would cater for the heavy traffic, leaving more room in the centre for shoppers. Everyone agreed this was an excellent idea which should be put into action without delay. Mr. Higginbottom put the job out to tender and in due course received several quotations. On reviewing them he was pleased to find one of the quotes was much cheaper than all the others. However, there was a snag: in order for it to be built at this reduced price the road would have to go through the spot where Biddy O'Flaherty's shop now stood, which meant that building would have to be completely demolished and the old lady provided with alternative accommodation.

Being a skinflint who didn't like spending the council's money any more than his own, Mr. Higginbottom was eager to go ahead with the job at the reduced rate. This meant he'd have to inform Biddy of the council's decision and hopefully she wouldn't take it too badly. The following Monday evening Biddy was dozing by the fire after her day's work when she heard a knock on the door. When she opened it she was surprised to see a gentleman in a suit standing there on her doorstep with a briefcase in his hand.

"Good evening Ms. O'Flaherty. I'm James Higginbottom from the town council. Could I have a word with you?"

"Of course, come in out of the cold."

Mr. Higginbottom entered Biddy's cosy kitchen and sat down. Then he opened his brief case and took out some papers which he spread on the table in front of him. Now that he was here in Biddy's house he felt distinctly uncomfortable. How was he going to break the news to her and, more importantly, how would she react? There was nothing for it, he told himself, but to take the bull by the horns and come straight out with it, so he cleared his throat and began.

Sitting back in her comfortable, old armchair and feeling drowsy from the heat of the fire, Biddy closed her eyes as she listened to the man from the council droning on about how they were going to knock down her house and she'd have to go live in a nursing home. Wouldn't it be terrible, she thought, if that happened in real life; thank God it's only a dream! When he finished speaking Mr. Higginbottom glanced in Biddy's direction to see if there was any reaction. When he saw her sitting there with her eyes closed he was appalled. Had the woman been listening at all, or was he talking to himself?

"Ms. O'Flaherty," he continued in a voice loud enough now to wake the dead, "What do you think of my proposal?"

Biddy opened her eyes and looked around. This was no dream; it was real! Suddenly, she was shaking with indignation.

"How dare you come here and tell me

you're going to knock down my house and put me in a nursing home."

"Well, we thought a nursing home would be best for you on account of your age, you're not getting any younger you know."

"So you know what's best for me, do you? Well, you listen to me, Mr. Higginbottom. If you bring a bulldozer here to knock down my house, the only way you can do it is with me inside of it because I'm telling you here and now I'm going nowhere. And that's my final word on the matter." Grabbing the poker she made a vicious stab at the fire. "And now I'd like you to leave."

Mr. Higginbottom didn't have to be told a second time. He didn't like the look in Biddy's eye, or the way she was handling the poker. Without another word he grabbed his papers, stuffed them into the briefcase and made a beeline for the door. As soon as he got outside he breathed a sigh of relief; he mightn't have made much progress with Ms. O'Flaherty that evening, but at least he'd gotten away with his life.

After that several attempts were made to

get Biddy to come to some sort of agreement with the council. They even offered to give her a house in a different part of town which she blankly refused. In the end it was decided the job would go ahead in a month's time, and hopefully, she'd change her mind before the work actually began.

It wasn't long until word spread in the locality about the dilemma now facing Biddy. The children were especially upset as they couldn't imagine coming home from school in the evening without dropping into her little shop for their sweets and ice cream. But it wasn't just the children, the adults were equally unhappy at the news. They all agreed that building a ring road would be good for the town, but not at the expense of destroying Biddy's home and livelihood. Something would have to be done. Without further delay a few of Biddy's closest neighbours got together and devised a plan which they hoped would work to save the day. Everything had to be done under cover as it wouldn't do for Mr. Higginbottom or his cohorts in the council to get wind of what they were planning.

Towards the end of June Biddy received a letter informing her that the contractor would arrive at eight o'clock sharp on Monday morning, the fifth of July, to demolish her premises. She was strongly advised to have vacated the building and taken all her possessions with her before that date. Biddy, of course, took no action whatsoever; she wasn't going anywhere.

On the morning of the appointed day, Biddy got up at seven o'clock and had her breakfast as usual. At a quarter to eight she went into the shop, which was at the front of the house and looked out through the window. Just like any other morning in summer, the sun was shining and all was peaceful outside. As she looked down the road there was no sign of the dreaded machinery on its way, but she did notice something else. Making its way up the road in her direction was a steady stream of people. When they reached her premises they stopped and began to form a queue outside the shop door. As she stood there trying to figure out what was going on, more and more people arrived, and it wasn't long until the queue stretched from her door all the way down the road and around the bend. When she opened the door Biddy saw that her nearest neighbour, Jack Ryan, was the first man in the queue.

"What's going on Jack?" she asked as he followed her into the shop.

"Well, it's like this Biddy," he replied, "as long as you have a queue of customers outside your shop, the men with the machinery won't be able to do a thing. They can hardly drive over innocent men, women and children to get to your premises, now can they?"

"That's a wonderful idea Jack, but how long will the queue last for?"

"It'll last for as long as is necessary, we won't be giving up until we know the council have changed their plans."

And that was exactly what happened. When the workmen arrived they waited for an hour or so to see if the queue would come to an end, and when it didn't, they left. The same thing happened every day that week. Mr.

Higginbottom was livid. He sent for the police to see if they could disperse the crowd but to no avail. The police explained that, as long as Ms. O'Flaherty had a license to sell goods and there were customers queuing up to buy them, there was nothing they could do; no law was being broken. In the end the council abandoned the idea of demolishing Biddy's premises altogether and the plans for the ring road had to be changed accordingly.

Biddy was overwhelmed by all the support she had received from her customers whom she now realised were also her friends, and she was happy to continue serving them in her little shop for a long time to come. As for Mr. Higginbottom, his tenure on the town council was cut short as he received pitifully few votes in the next election. Shortly afterwards he left Doonmore and was never seen or heard of in that part of the country again.

THE PROMISE

Eddie O'Sullivan lived with his parents in a tiny cottage in a remote part of the country. At twelve years old he was small for his age and could pass for a boy of nine or ten which often led to teasing and bullying by bigger boys with whom he attended the local school. On the way to school they had to pass by a large estate belonging to a wealthy gentleman,

Mr. Smith. Most of the boys had never seen Mr. Smith in person as he didn't mix with the local people whom he considered beneath him. There was, however, one thing they did know about him and that was that he had a magnificent orchard. Every year he won first prize for his apples at the annual horticultural show which was held in the nearby town, and his picture was often seen in the local newspaper.

One evening when Eddie and three other boys were passing by the estate, one of them suggested that they should raid Mr. Smith's orchard and sample for themselves some of those gorgeous, prizewinning apples. The others agreed it was a brilliant idea and, not wanting to be seen as a coward, Eddie said he'd go along with them. Without further delay they climbed over the wall and soon they were stuffing their schoolbags and pockets with the delicious-looking, juicy, red fruit. For a while everything was quiet, but suddenly, they heard barking and there was Mr. Smith hurrying through the trees towards them accompanied by two fierce looking dogs.

"Run! Run!" someone shouted and grabbing their schoolbags they took off like the wind towards the outer wall. The three bigger lads managed to climb up and over the top just in time, but Eddie wasn't so lucky. He had just managed to get his feet off the ground and thought he might make it, when he felt a hand grab his jacket and pull him back down. Mr. Smith dragged him up to the house, bundled him into his car and drove him down to the garda station in the village. When he had explained the situation to Sergeant Delaney, Mr. Smith left him to do his job. The Sergeant brought Eddie into the office and told him to take a seat. Then, taking out a notebook and pen, he began to question him.

"What's your name?"
"Eddie O'Sullivan, Sergeant.
"Did you enter Mr. Smith's orchard this afternoon for the purpose of stealing apples?"
"Yes, Sergeant."
"Was there anyone else with you?"
"There were three others, Peter Riley, Sean

Dempsey and … and … Seamus Delaney."

The Sergeant looked up sharply from the notebook where he'd been writing. "You mean my son, Seamus?"

"Yes Sergeant. In fact, it was his idea, the rest of us just went along with him."

"Listen here now Eddie, I think you made a mistake. You went into that orchard by yourself, didn't you?"

"No Sergeant, I told you there were four of us."

"And I said you were on your own. Are you listening to me at all?" The sergeant was shouting now and his face was becoming a vivid shade of red.

"You want me to take all the blame, but that's not fair".

The sergeant was silent for a moment as he considered how best to deal with this situation.

"Tell me this Eddie," he said, leaning back in his chair and taking a long drag on his cigarette, "What does your father do for a living?"

Now, there were a couple of possible answers

to this question, and Eddie wasn't sure which was most appropriate on this occasion,

"Hmm, he's on the dole."

"And why is he on the dole?"

"B-because he can't get a job."

"Ah, but that's the problem. You know as well as I do that he's been working for years with certain farmers around this district. Being the decent sort that I am, I never said anything about his double dealings before. However, if I were to report him to the authorities he'd do a spell in jail; there's no doubt about that."

When Eddie heard this he was horrified. He couldn't bear the thought of his father going to jail. He sat there silently looking down at the floor.

"So Now Eddie, I'm going to ask you again. Was there anyone with you in Mr. Smith's orchard today?"

"No Sergeant, I was on my own," mumbled Eddie, as he continued to stare at the floor.

"Good" smiled the Sergeant smugly, "And remember, as long as you stick to that version of events, your father won't get into any trouble. Now, off you go and you'll be hearing from me again before long."

At the next sitting of the district court Eddie had to appear before a judge who sentenced him to three years in a detention center for juvenile delinquents which was situated over fifty miles away. Everyone thought this was a particularly harsh sentence for something as trivial as stealing apples. However, what most people didn't know was that the judge owed a debt to Mr. Smith for a favour he'd done him in the past. So, in order to keep that gentleman happy, someone had to pay the price and, unfortunately, that someone was Eddie.

The first few months away from home were the worst, as he felt homesick all the time and had trouble adjusting to his new surroundings. However, there was one thing that kept him going, and that was the carpentry workshop where he showed great aptitude for the work. Every term he won first prize for his projects, and before he left he became the proud recipient of a certificate which proclaimed that he was a qualified carpenter.

When Eddie finally returned home he thought he'd have no bother getting a job in the area. However, he was bitterly disappointed. As soon as prospective employers heard he'd spent the last three years in a detention centre, they came up with all kinds of excuses not to employ him. He continued on like this for two years, applying for jobs but always being turned down. When he was seventeen he decided he'd had enough; there was only one thing for it: he'd take the boat to England.

His parents were sad to see him leave for the second time, but they knew he had no choice. As things turned out, it was the best decision he could have made. He had no bother getting work in England where no one knew or cared about his past. He was a qualified carpenter and a good worker; that was all they needed to know about him. Eddie worked hard at his trade and eventually he set up his own business where he gave a start to several young Irish lads as they too tried to find their way in a new country. He married a girl from home and they had two sons who were now running the business with him. Now that he could afford to take some time off he made it his business to go home at least once a year to visit his parents.

When he was almost thirty years in England, Eddie was in a pub one night enjoying a drink with some friends. While he was there, he noticed a shabbily dressed, gaunt-faced man sitting alone at the bar staring into his drink. He thought he looked familiar, but he couldn't figure out where he'd seen him before. Later in the evening, however, it came to him: he was Seamus Delaney, the sergeant's son, who had been the ringleader in the raid on Mr. Smith's orchard all those years ago. Out of curiosity more than anything else, Eddie went over to speak to him.

"Hello Seamus,"
Seamus turned and looked blankly at him.
"Hello," he mumbled, "do I know you?"
"You should know me," replied Eddie, "We went to school together, I'm Eddie O'Sullivan."

Seamus Delaney's face turned even whiter than it had been. In fact, he looked like someone who'd just seen a ghost. "E-eddie O'Sullivan?" he stammered. I didn't think I'd ever see you again. I'm surprised you're even speaking to me after the way my father treated you."

"I was treated badly alright, but I never considered it your fault."

"That's very decent of you Eddie," declared Seamus, as the two men shook hands. "I've often thought about what happened and wondered how things worked out for you. I'm glad to see that you have the appearance of a man who has done well for himself in spite of everything."

"All things considered, I suppose I haven't done too badly," agreed Eddie.

The same, unfortunately, couldn't be said for Seamus. Before they left the pub that night he brought Eddie up to date on the story of his life since he arrived in England. After years of drinking which ruined his health and left him penniless, he was now living alone in a tiny bedsit with only a bottle for company.

"Do you ever go home to see your parents?" asked Eddie.

"No, I lost contact with them years ago; they have no idea whether I'm dead or alive.

"It's not too late yet; perhaps you could still visit them."

Seamus looked at him sadly. "Ah, but that's the thing, Eddie; it *is* too late! I know, as sure as I'm sitting here on this barstool, I'll never set foot in Ireland again."

For the next half hour the two old school pals chatted about everything and anything and before they knew it the barman was shouting "time gentlemen please". They said their goodbyes and as Eddie walked away to join his friends, Seamus suddenly called him back.

"Could you do me a favour?"

"What is it?"

"The next time you go home would you call to my parents and give them a message from me. J-just tell them I'm doing well over here; I'm busy at the moment, but I'll be home to see them the first chance I get."

" I'll make sure they get that message."

Seamus grasped Eddie's hand and held it tightly as his eyes filled with tears. "Thanks Eddie, you don't know how much that means to me." Then, letting go of his old school pal's hand, and, in all likelihood, the last link to his past, he turned slowly back to his unfinished drink.

The months passed and Eddie was busy getting on with his life. It was only when he was on the plane taking him across the Irish Sea again, that he remembered the promise he had made to Seamus. Now that he had time to think about it, he realised that the last thing he wanted to do was speak to Sergeant Delaney again; that man treated him despicably when he was a vulnerable child, so why should he do him any favours now? Perhaps he should just forget about the whole thing; nobody would be any the wiser. Then he thought of how Seamus had grasped his hand and the tears of gratitude in his eyes, and he knew that no matter how unpleasant it might be to come face to face with the sergeant again, he couldn't let it stop him from fulfilling a promise made to an old school pal who was down on his luck.

ABOUT THE AUTHOR

Mary Nolan lives near Borris in County Carlow. She loves reading and writing about life in rural Ireland in times gone by. Mary completed a Creative Writing Course at The People's College, Dublin in 2019 and has had her work published in books and magazines.

Other Books Available

The Deserted Cottage
A Good Neighbour
New Beginnings
Time to Go Home
The Hannigan Sisters

Contact Details:
Email: marynolan73517@gmail.com
Phone No: 086 3451716

Printed in Great Britain
by Amazon